"No," he rasped savagely, withdrawing from her

"What's the matter, Rafe?" Brooke controlled her sudden, sickening relief. "Did you close your eyes again and imagine I was your wife?"

He had paled to a ghastly gray, his eyes tormented black pools. "Brooke—"

"Would you just leave?" She turned away, to hide the fear she felt.

"I don't…I can't—"

"Will you just go!"

"Am I to be haunted by her for the rest of my life?" he groaned, as he slowly let himself out of the cottage, leaving a devastated Brooke behind him.

Even physically changed as she was, Rafe's body persisted in recognizing her. How long before his mind knew her, too?

Books by Carole Mortimer

HARLEQUIN PRESENTS

These books may be available at your local bookseller.

For a list of all titles currently available,
send your name and address to:

Harlequin Reader Service
P.O. Box 52040, Phoenix, AZ 85072-2040
Canadian address: P.O. Box 2800, Postal Station A,
5170 Yonge St., Willowdale, Ont. M2N 5T5

CAROLE MORTIMER

a lost love

Harlequin Books

TORONTO • NEW YORK • LONDON
AMSTERDAM • PARIS • SYDNEY • HAMBURG
STOCKHOLM • ATHENS • TOKYO • MILAN

For
John and Matthew

———◆—◆—◆———

Harlequin Presents first edition November 1984
ISBN 0-373-10740-4

Original hardcover edition published in 1984
by Mills & Boon Limited

CHAPTER ONE

BROOKE looked at the palely fragile woman who lay back against the white bedclothes, her heart constricting in her throat at how much more ill the other woman looked since the last time she had visited her—and that had only been yesterday! Dear Jocelyn, how bravely she was handling the fatal illness that had suddenly afflicted her six months ago, the last month of it spent in this private nursing-home; she seemed to grow weaker and more frail with each passing day.

It made Brooke angry that the other woman, the best friend she had ever had, should have to suffer such pain, that she herself should feel so helpless in the face of Jocelyn's unspoken suffering.

To look at the two of them they had little in common; Jocelyn was in her sixties, Brooke in her early twenties. The older woman's face showed signs of a faded beauty, while the younger had an exquisitely beautiful face that required little make-up, just a light brown mascara to darken the blonde lashes that surrounded shadowed blue eyes, a deep red lipgloss outlining the perfect curve of her mouth. The older woman's hair had gone gracefully grey years earlier, the younger woman having a light brown colour with blonde highlights in the thick shoulder-length swathe of straight hair.

And yet during the last three years it had been Jocelyn who had become Brooke's confidante when she needed her so much, developing what could only be called a mother–daughter relationship, as they spent a great deal of time together, Jocelyn never having married and Brooke's parents having died long ago.

7

Brooke knew that the Charlwoods, Jocely[...]
viewed the friendship with some scepticism,[...]
Brooke obviously had wealth of her own they[...]
been able to accuse her of being after the[...]
woman's money. But both of them knew that[...]
friendship was frowned upon by the head of[...]
Charlwood family, Rafe, his brother Patrick and h[...]
wife Rosemary. But Jocelyn had never been influence[...]
by the opinion of either of her nephews, nor their fathe[...]
either when he had been alive, and so the friendship ha[...]
continued to flourish, Brooke visiting Jocelyn at he[...]
cottage on the Charlwood estate whenever she could
To their credit the attitude of the Charlwood family ha[...]
been consistent as far as Brooke was concerned—the[...]
ignored her existence wherever possible.

And that was the way she wanted it, preferring not t[...]
have attention brought to her, especially in front o[...]
Rafe, the powerful head of the family and o[...]
Charlwood Industries, a man who was as harsh as h[...]
was wealthy. The family had amassed even more mone[...]
under his guidance than when Robert Charlwood[...]
Rafe's great-grandfather, had begun their first shippin[...]
line all those years ago. Brooke knew the whole histor[...]
of the Charlwood family, had met several of them, an[...]
the only one she had ever liked had been Jocelyn.

'Are you angry with the flowers, darling, or me?[...]
Jocelyn teased her from her sitting position in the be[...]
in this sunlit room that looked little like a nursing-hom[...]
and more like a woman's boudoir, soft and feminine, a[...]
was the woman in the bed, her pretty pink bed-jacke[...]
matching her lace nightgown.

Brooke had to blink back the tears as she looked a[...]
her friend, the carnations she had been arranging in th[...]
vase forgotten for the moment. 'Neither,' she choked
'I'm angry at life. Why you, Jocelyn?' she groaned he[...]
despair. 'Why not me, when I——'

'It isn't for us to question that,' the other woma[...]

gently rebuked. 'Everything has a purpose. And I think I know what mine is,' she added softly, patting the bed at her side. 'Come and sit here, I want to talk to you.'

The sheer intensity of Jocelyn's voice when she was feeling so ill was enough to send Brooke across the room to sit on the bedside. 'Is there anything wrong?' she asked worriedly. 'The tests you had at the beginning of the week . . .?'

'Just confirmed what I already knew,' the other woman patted her hand comfortingly. 'I shan't last the month.'

'You mustn't talk that way!' Brooke blanched, her hand tightening about her friend's. 'There are so many things they can do now, medical science is advancing every day.'

Jocelyn shook her head, her smile serene. 'They told me at the beginning that my illness was inoperable, and science isn't moving quick enough for me. I've accepted it, darling. I wish you would.'

'I know,' Brooke's bottom lip trembled. 'And it's selfish of me to feel this way when your pain is so bad. But what am I going to do without you?' She held the other woman's hand up to her cheek, her tears falling unchecked now.

Jocelyn gave a sad smile, smoothing the damp cheek with her fingertips. 'You'll survive,' she assured her gently. 'And I've made provision for you in my will——'

'No!' Brooke raised stricken eyes, huge limpid blue eyes that reflected the fear in her heart. 'I don't want anything, don't need anything, you know that. And it will just make Rafe—the family—dislike me more.'

'I'm not doing this just for you.' The older woman held her gaze. 'This has always involved more than just you and me, that's why I allowed things to go as far as they did.' She gave a deep sigh. 'Rafe is a hard, unforgiving man, there was no other way. But I haven't

left you any money, Brooke, we both know there's little
need for that,' she added wryly. 'And as you say, the
family already dislikes you enough.'

Brooke frowned her puzzlement. 'If not money then
what . . .?'

'You'll soon see.' Jocelyn gave a tight smile. 'And
don't think I didn't give it all a great deal of thought
before I did it, because I did.'

'I would feel easier in my mind if I knew what "it"
is,' Brooke sighed.

'You'll know all in good time,' she was assured. 'My
lawyer will contact you at the appropriate time.'

'When you're dead,' Brooke said flatly.

'Now, now, dear, we all have to go some time,'
Jocelyn smiled. 'I've had a good life, a happy one. And
now I want to try and give you a little happiness
too——'

'Your dying couldn't do that!' Brooke choked.

'None of us wish for my aunt's death, Miss
Adamson,' rasped a deeply harsh voice. 'I'm sure none
of us wish to even consider it.'

The sound of that voice brought Brooke to her feet,
her face averted as she wiped away all trace of her
recent tears, not needing to look at the man who had
just entered the room to know who he was: Rafe
Charlwood, head of the Charlwood family. Thirty-nine
years old, dark hair liberally sprinkled with grey at his
temples, a harsh face seeming as if carved from granite,
the eyes a light steady grey, his nose long and straight,
flanked by high cheekbones and lean cheeks, a firm
uncompromsing mouth, his chin square and strong, his
jaw determined. His body was lean, his height immense,
and yet he possessed a certain elegance of movement, a
feline grace in the wide shoulders, tapered waist, narrow
hips, and long legs. Brooke knew all that about the man
without even looking at him, hating to look at him,
remembering then all the pain he had caused her in the

past. And such was this man's arrogance, his fiercely possessive vengeance, that he hadn't even known he had wronged her.

Jocelyn shot Brooke an understanding glance before concentrating on her nephew. 'You may not want to discuss it, Rafe,' she said softly, 'but I can assure you it's going to happen. Now tell me what you're doing here?' she demanded. 'I thought you were going to Italy for the next few weeks.'

He shrugged, moving forward to kiss her dutifully on one powdered cheek, as sophisticated as usual in an elegant charcoal-grey three-piece suit and silver-grey shirt and tie, both of the latter looking like silk. 'I concluded my business early,' he dismissed, 'so I thought I would pay you a visit.' The steely gaze was once more turned on Brooke. 'I had no idea Miss Adamson was going to be here.'

Brooke hadn't needed to be told that; she knew that if he had realised he would have arranged for his own visit not to have coincided with hers. It was his lack of effort to hide his disapproval of her that had influenced his young brother Patrick into feeling the same way, and his sister-in-law needed no encouragement in that direction; her reaction was hostile on sight.

'Brooke comes to see me most afternoons.' His aunt spoke conversationally, although she was well aware of the tension between her friend and her nephew, preferring to ignore it rather than argue against it, as she had once tried to do. She knew Rafe well enough to know that once he decided on something, in this case that he disliked and distrusted Brooke, then nothing would change his mind.

Brooke disliked and distrusted him too—worse than that, she feared him; knew of the cruelty inside him that governed his own actions and those closest to him, mainly Patrick and Rosemary Charlwood. Whatever Rafe said went, as far as all of the family were concerned. Even though Jocelyn stood up to him or occasion she still accepted that Rafe was the head of th family, that he ran the business with precision skil' adding to the family fortune every day that he heade the company.

Brooke had never been able to understand thi family's blind acceptance of one man's will, and sh avoided meeting Rafe Charlwood whenever possibl Unfortunately, as Jocelyn had already pointed ou' neither of them had expected him here today. If the had Brooke would have suitably absented herself. As was, she would now have to brazen this meeting out– and make her excuses to leave as soon as possible.

'Indeed?' Hard grey eyes studied her across the widt of the bed as he answered his aunt.

She turned fully to face him, meeting his gaz steadily, unflinching as his mouth twisted in derision perfectly able to guess at the antagonism she felt in h sensed mockery. Clear blue eyes warred with steely gre ones, and it was hard to say who would have been th first to look away if Jocelyn hadn't softly interrupte the silent battle, drawing her nephew's attention back t her.

'How are the family?' she asked lightly.

Rafe looked down at the elderly woman from h imposing height, his thick dark hair styled low over h ears and collar in a casually windswept look that wa nevertheless expensively cut—like the rest of hin 'Didn't Patrick and Rosemary visit you only th morning?' he drawled.

Jocelyn flushed. 'They don't happen to be the who family,' she said waspishly.

His mouth firmed. 'If you want to know how Robe is then why not come right out and ask?'

Brooke's temper rose in indignation at the way h spoke to his aunt.

But she needn't have been concerned for Jocelyn. Tl

other woman hadn't reached her sixty-fifth year, remained unmarried, without learning to stand up for herself against the Charlwood men, Rafe most of all, if she felt strongly about something. 'I shouldn't need to ask, Rafe,' she snapped. 'He is the only great-nephew I have.'

'And likely to remain so,' the man at her side bit out.

Brooke's sharp gaze raked over the sudden tightness of his face as he talked about his son. Dear God, Robert was only three years old—how could he have evoked such a tight-lipped response from his own father? Was the man completely inhuman?

'Well?' Jocelyn demanded.

Rafe gave an arrogant inclination of his head, disapproval of being spoken to in this way emanating from each tautly held line of his body. 'Robert is very well.'

'Did you take him to Italy with you?' his aunt probed.

'He stayed at Charlwood with Nanny Perkins.'

'As usual,' his aunt said disapprovingly. 'You really don't see enough of the boy, Rafe. He needs his father——'

'I don't believe that's something that should be discussed now, Jocelyn.' His softly spoken words cut her off effectively, the edge to his voice ominously clear.

But Jocelyn didn't heed that warning, having lived through too many decades of the harsh authority of the Charlwood men to listen to it from her nephew. 'Because of Brooke?' she dismissed impatiently. 'It isn't exactly a secret that you neglect your son, and after you fought so fiercely for custody of him too.'

Rafe shot Brooke a resentful glance, although his voice remained controlled. 'I fought for my son for the simple reason that my wife was an unfit mother for him.' His narrow-eyed gaze returned to Brooke as he heard her gasp. 'Don't act so surprised, Miss

Adamson,' he mocked abruptly. 'The sensation of my much-publicised separation from my wife two and a half years ago is often held up by the press as an example to less wary men of wealth when they find themselves attracted to a totally unsuitable woman.' Contempt curled his top lip. 'My wife was a dancer when we met, Miss Adamson, did you know that?'

As he said, she knew all about his much-publicised marriage, the nine-day wonder of the way he had exposed his wife's infidelity to the court and public alike in an effort to gain custody of their only child at their separation, a baby of only six months at the time. At least the little boy had been too young to know of his mother's humiliation and consequent death. And considering the way this man had exposed his private life then, admitted to the mistake he had made in marrying the nineteen-year-old dancer, he seemed to care little for the son he had wanted so desperately to keep, and left the child mainly to the care of his nanny.

'Oh, not ballet or classical,' Rafe Charlwood derided himself. 'She belonged to a group of modern dancers who appeared on the Greg Davieson show—they were called Sensuous Romance,' he added distastefully.

'I remember them,' Brooke nodded woodenly.

His hands tightened momentarily into fists before he seemed visibly to force himself to relax, smiling without humour. 'Then you will also remember that my wife found Mr Davieson more attractive than our marriage.'

'Don't you mean than you?' Brooke bit down painfully on her bottom lip as his rapier-sharp gaze ripped into her with barely controlled anger. 'I'm sorry,' she muttered, looking down at her clasped hands. 'I shouldn't have said that.'

'Why not?' he scorned harshly. 'You're exactly right, Miss Adamson,' he bit out grimly. 'My wife did indeed find Greg Davieson more attractive than me.'

'I'm sure Brooke doesn't want to hear all this, Rafe——

'Why not?' he coldly interrupted his aunt. 'I'm sure Miss Adamson isn't so innocent that the fact that my wife had an affair with another man would shock her.'

'Rafe——'

'It's all right, Jocelyn,' Brooke soothed the other woman as she looked like becoming agitated by the exchange. 'Mr Charlwood and I are just—talking.' She turned back to him, having to bend her head back slightly to meet his gaze despite her own height of five feet eight, the three-inch heels on her black sandals even adding to this. 'I'm not shocked by your wife's behaviour at all, Mr Charlwood, although I would be very surprised if the breakdown of your marriage rested solely with her. You see, I too have been married,' she continued despite his icy grey eyes chilling over even more, watching now as his gaze moved to her ringless hands. Her mouth twisted with derision for that look. 'One doesn't have to wear a ring to bear the scars of a marriage,' she told him tautly. 'Those you carry inside you—for ever,' she added bitterly.

His head moved questioningly to one side, a slightly puzzled look on the arrogantly self-assured face. 'I had no idea you had been married—are married?'

'Was,' she corrected abruptly.

'Then you aren't Miss Adamson at all . . .'

'I am,' she told him sharply. 'It isn't unusual for a woman to revert to her maiden name once a marriage is over.'

'And your husband?' Rafe Charlwood eyes were narrowed. 'Where is he?'

For a moment she hesitated, breathing deeply. 'Like your wife, he's dead,' she finally stated flatly. 'Yes, he's dead,' she repeated more confidently, and turned with a gasp of dismay as she heard Jocelyn give a choked cry, bending over the other woman concernedly as she saw how pale she had become. 'I'm sorry, Jocelyn,' she groaned her remorse. 'Our conversation has upset you.'

Her eyes pleaded with the other woman for her understanding, knowing it was given by the compassionate look in her friend's eyes. 'You're looking tired,' she squeezed Jocelyn's hand between both her own. 'I'll leave you to rest now.'

'I'll leave with you.' Rafe Charlwood straightened to his full height of well over six feet.

Brooke gave him a stricken look, bending down to kiss Jocelyn goodbye before turning to pick up her clutch-bag from the coffee table in front of the Regency-style sofa, her figure as slender as that of a model, wearing a cream and black silk dress with an elegance that also spoke of professional training, moving with unconscious grace. 'I'm sure you would rather stay and talk to your aunt privately for a few minutes,' she gave him a cool meaningless smile. 'I'll come and see you again tomorrow, Jocelyn.' Her voice warmed noticeably.

'You mustn't waste all your time on an old woman,' she was instantly scolded. 'I won't mind if you miss one day.'

'But I would,' Brooke rebuked gently. 'It's my time Jocelyn, and nothing pleases me more than visiting you. Can I bring you anything?'

'Maybe an Agatha Christie?' the other woman requested hopefully. 'I like a good mystery novel.'

Brooke gave a light laugh. 'I'll hunt around for one you haven't read,' she lightly mocked the stack of books that had already accumulated on the bedside table, ignoring the cynicism she sensed emanating from the silent Rafe Charlwood. 'You'll soon be able to start your own library,' she teased.

Jocelyn gave a rueful smile of acknowledgment of the fact. 'You've been very good to me——'

'It's no more than you deserve,' she hastily cut in on the words of gratitude, knowing that Rafe Charlwood's scorn was growing by the second. 'Same time tomorrow, hmm?' she prompted lightly.

'Lovely,' her friend smiled.

'Mr Charlwood,' Brooke gave him a cold nod of dismissal, knowing by the hard glitter of his eyes that it wasn't something he was used to. Well, she didn't give a damn about what he liked or disliked, the only person she cared about in this room was Jocelyn and the help she had given her both now and in the past, and it was for that reason and that reason alone that she had been able to control her temper earlier when it had threatened to spill over into anger.

She began to breathe easier as soon as she left the private room, the heels on her sandals clattering noisily as she walked down the quiet corridor, out of the door at the end and into the sunshine. Strange, while she had been confined in the room with the oppressive presence of Rafe Charlwood she had forgotten it was a bright and sunny day in mid-August. There was a beautiful picturesque garden outside the clinic, and Brooke took a few minutes to breathe in the enchantment of a sea of multi-coloured flowers, listening to the soothing sound of the birds singing overhead in the lush green trees.

'Waiting for me?' drawled a familiar voice, heavily veiled with sarcasm now.

Had she been, even subconsciously? No, definitely not, came back the unequivocable answer. 'Not at all, Mr Charlwood,' she replied stiffly, turning to face him, clinically noting how the bright sunshine made his hair appear almost black, the wings of lighter hair at his temples silver. He had a deep tan out here in the sunshine, as if he had recently been on holiday. Perhaps all his time in Italy hadn't been spent working?

He strolled over to join her, moving with lithe grace, the dark suit strangely formal for a visit to the aunt he was so fond of. He seemed aware of her disapproval. 'I came here straight from the airport,' he explained mockingly.

'What a busy man you are!' She turned to begin

walking to her car which was parked a short distance away, feeling irritation as he fell into step beside her, the grey matallic and black Rolls-Royce that he drove parked next to her dark green Porsche.

'And you,' he drawled. 'What do you do when you aren't visiting sick friends in hospital?'

Her fingers curved about her bag, the long nails that were painted the same deep red as her lipgloss digging into the fine leather. 'Nothing,' she stated abruptly. 'But then there have to be people like me to give people like you an example *not* to follow.' She arched dark blonde brows at him in challenge.

For a moment he looked perplexed by the acidity of her tone, then his expression became bland once again. 'You don't like me, do you?' he said conversationally.

Brooke almost sighed her relief as she reached her car, unlocking the door with quick, fluid movements and sliding gratefully behind the wheel. 'I think you have that the wrong way round, Mr Charlwood.' She closed her door, turning on the ignition to press the button that would automatically open the window next to her and turning to look at him. 'It's you who doesn't like me.'

He leant back against his car as it stood only a couple of feet away in this almost-full car park. 'I don't know you,' his mouth quirked. 'It's hard to dislike someone you don't know.'

Brooke tossed the straight thickness of her sun-bleached hair over her shoulder. 'Then let's just say you give a very good impression of it,' she said with saccharine sweetness, revving the engine pointedly as she began to reverse her car away from him.

In two strides he had caught up with her, his hands on the frame of the open window at her side making it impossible for her to move the car back any further. 'Maybe I do,' he conceded abruptly. 'And maybe we should do something about it. Will you have dinner with me tonight?'

Her eyes widened with suspicion. She didn't trust this man, had good reason not to do so. Her mouth tightened. 'Why don't you go home and spend some time with your son, Mr Charlwood?' she rasped contemptuously. 'You don't sound as if you know him either!' Her foot stepped down on the accelerator, not caring now that he still stood dangerously close to the car, her last sight of him as she glanced in the driving mirror and saw him looking after her with coldly vengeful eyes.

That last comment about his son had been stupid and reckless, had assuredly alienated a man she knew to be cruel and vicious. But he was also a man she couldn't afford to become close to, a man that she hated, and feared, with all her heart.

Jocelyn seemed much worse in succeeding days, her vitality draining quickly, her wanderings into the past becoming more and more frequent, although she was aware of what was happening at these times, simply regretting mistakes made in a youth that had been long gone.

Brooke listened with fascination to the tales Jocelyn told her of life at Charlwood when she was a child, of the grand parties given there, which she had only been allowed to witness from illicit looks from upstairs.

'It was wonderful to grow up there.' Jocelyn lay back weakly on the pillows, tiring more and more easily now. A troubled frown marred her brow. 'I wish Robert could enjoy it the way I did.' She sighed. 'Rafe wanted to bring him in to see me——'

'Here?' Brooke gave a dismayed gasp.

She nodded. 'I told him how ridiculous he was being. A three-year-old shouldn't have to see his Aunt Jossy lying here looking helpless—and feeling it.'

'No,' Brooke absently toyed with the pattern on the pink candlewick bedspread. She hadn't seen Rafe

Charlwood since that last troubled incident, although it seemed he had visited his aunt recently.

'I managed to persuade him that a hospital is no place for an impressionable child,' Jocelyn told her with satisfaction.

'Persuade?' she mocked.

'I *forbade* him,' Jocelyn corrected with a trace of her old imperiousness. 'He's too hard on the boy,' she muttered. 'Expects too much of him; he's still only a baby.' Her face softened as she thought of her great-nephew.

Brooke knew how much Jocelyn loved the little boy, a tall boy for only three years of age, with his father's dark hair and clearly defined features, although his eyes were a warm blue. Brooke had met the little boy several times herself when visiting Jocelyn at her cottage on the estate, Robert being a constant visitor to his Aunty Jossy, seeming to enjoy the informality and fun to be found at her home. As yet Brooke could see no effect on the little boy from his father's strict and often harsh attitude towards him, but one day it would come, the nervousness, the fear, and when that day did come Rafe Charlwood would have lost his son's love as surely as he had once lost his wife's.

'It isn't wise to antagonise Rafe.' Jocelyn sensed Brooke's resentment. 'He's more powerful than all of us.'

Brooke repressed a shudder. 'I know that,' she said dully. 'But that's no reason to be a tyrant to a little boy who can't stand up for himself.'

'He isn't a tyrant,' the other woman shook her head. 'He loves the boy, but he just can't show it, doesn't like to show any sign of weakness. He was hurt and disillusioned once, but he has no intention of repeating the experience.'

'With his own son?' Brooke scorned. 'There's no shame attached to loving one's child, in loving him so desperately that you'll do anything, be anything, to be with him.' She spoke with a vehemence of feeling that made her voice quiver.

Jocelyn squeezed her hand to help lessen the pain. 'I'm so sorry things didn't work out for you, darling,' she sympathised gently. 'It's so difficult——'

'Please don't worry about it,' she hastened to reassure the other woman, knowing that fretting about her problems was the last thing Jocelyn needed. 'I'll manage.'

'I know you will,' her friend nodded, giving a regretful sigh. 'You're a very strong-minded young lady. It's a pity——'

'Please, Jocelyn,' she said tightly. 'There's no point in talking about it.'

'No. But my will,' Jocelyn went on insistently. 'You won't oppose it?'

Brooke sighed, not wanting to upset her friend, but not wanting anything from her will either. The subject hadn't been discussed since the day Rafe Charlwood had arrived so unexpectedly at the clinic, and she looked about her almost guiltily now, half expecting him to overhear and misunderstand the situation a second time. It was something he was good at!

'He's away.' Jocelyn's mouth quirked as she correctly guessed Brooke's haunted thoughts.

'Again?' Brooke's brows rose reproachfully.

'America this time,' the other woman nodded. 'For forty-eight hours, he said.' She gave a rueful smile. 'And God help anyone who delays him over that time! His work schedule would kill other men,' she shook her head, 'but Rafe actually seems to thrive on it.'

'And Robert?'

'He's quite happy with his nanny, happier than he should be if the truth were known.' Jocelyn shook her head sadly. 'It isn't the way it should be.'

'Rafe wanted his son,' Brooke bit out tautly.

'Because he felt Robert's mother was unfit to bring him up,' Jocelyn told her evenly.

'And was she?' Brooke scorned.

'I never thought so.'

'But Rafe did!'

Jocelyn shrugged. 'He believed he knew his wife. And we'll never know for sure now, not when Jacqui has been dead for two years. But I do know that Rafe will never give up his son, not to anyone.'

'What if he marries again?'

Jocelyn's reply was emphatic. 'That will never happen. My will, Brooke—you didn't answer me,' she prompted insistently.

Brooke sighed at the reintroduction of the subject she had been trying to avoid. 'It isn't money?' she asked warily.

'No,' came the assured answer.

'Then I suppose it will be all right,' Brooke said slowly.

'Thank you, dear.' Jocelyn closed her eyes tiredly. 'And don't be sad when I'm gone,' she murmured sleepily. 'Dying isn't so bad, it's living that can sometimes be so hard to do.'

Brooke knew that, knew all about the pain of living when what you really wanted to do was lie back and die . . .

It was a quiet funeral, the way Jocelyn would have wished it to be, just her close family and a few friends; the people who had really cared about her.

Jocelyn had died peacefully in the end, during her sleep, and after months of suffering it was the way she deserved to go. Brooke had received a terse telephone call from Rafe Charlwood himself telling her of his aunt's death during the night. Perhaps because it was he who called Brooke managed to contain her initial grief, answering him coolly.

'When will the funeral be held?' she asked stiltedly.

'The arrangements haven't been made yet,' he told her smoothly, showing little or no emotion himself, despite the fact that he had been very fond of his aunt. 'But I'm sure you would like to attend.'

'Of course.' Her tone was slightly defensive. Of course she wanted to attend; Jocelyn had been the best friend she had ever had, to desert her now would be disrespectful—even if the thought of going to Charlwood without her support terrified the life out of her!

'And I'm equally sure that Jocelyn would have wanted you to travel with the family——'

'No!' Her tone was sharp, and she sought to control that. 'I would rather drive myself, if you don't mind.'

There was silence for several minutes, as if Rafe Charlwood wasn't altogether pleased with her reply, but he knew there wasn't a damned thing he could do about it. Brooke was her own woman, financially independent, and Rafe Charlwood had no influence over her whatsoever—she wasn't even attracted to him, as she felt sure many other women would have been.

'If that's what you prefer,' he said coolly. 'You will, of course, come back to the house after the service.'

'I——'

'Our lawyer has requested that you do so, Miss Adamson,' he cut into her refusal. 'I believe your name will be mentioned in my aunt's will,' he added dryly.

The will! Dear God, she had forgotten her promise to Jocelyn about accepting the bequest in her will. But surely directly after a funeral was no time to read a will; it seemed positively macabre to Brooke.

'It's a family tradition,' Rafe Charlwood drawled as if reading her thoughts.

'I see.' Her tone capably conveyed her opinion that it was a tradition that should have been stopped years ago, although she gave no verbal opinion. 'In that case

I'll come back to Charlwood after the funeral. If that was all . . .?' she queried distantly.

'I'll call you.' Rafe Charlwood managed to convey his own feelings over the telephone just as capably—and he was coldly angry! 'As soon as I know the details,' he added abruptly.

'I would appreciate that.' She quickly rang off, realising that her control was about to slip. The shock of never seeing Jocelyn again was finally getting to her as Rafe Charlwood calmly discussed the 'arrangements'—almost as if those *arrangements* weren't the time and last resting place of one of the kindest, most understanding women Brooke had ever known.

She was going to miss Jocelyn more than she cared to think about; the other woman had been her one and only friend during the last few years, the only one she had dared to make. The future promised to be even more bleak than the last three years, but at least Jocelyn had been released from her pain, and Brooke could feel grateful for that.

As Rafe Charlwood approached her after the funeral she stood her ground, although as usual her first instinct was to turn and run. But none of her inner unbidden panic showed as she looked up at him with cool query, aware of the curious glances Rosemary Charlwood had given her before being persuaded by her husband to accompany him over to the waiting black limousines that would take the family back to the Charlwood estate.

Brooke stood pointedly beside her own car as Rafe Charlwood reached her side, wearing a brown suit tailored to her slenderness, a brown velvet hat covering the brightness of her hair. Rafe Charlwood was also suitably dressed in sombre clothing, having taken a day off from his business affairs to show his last respects to the woman who had helped his father bring up his brother and himself after his mother had died when he was a child. Maybe he was adept at hiding his feelings, but he didn't seem as heartbroken as Brooke knew herself to have been since he had telephoned her with the news of Jocelyn's death.

His icy gaze moved over her with cold appraisal—almost as if she were a well-bred racehorse being appraised for, and by, the prize stud. Brooke withstood that assessment with one of her own, at least having the satisfaction of knowing he hadn't defeated her with the silent battle of wills, although she knew by the mocking curve to his mouth that she hadn't been the victor either.

'Perhaps you could give me a lift back to the house?' he requested in that coolly clipped voice. 'That way I can direct you.'

Her own smile was tight, her eyes remaining hard. 'I know the way to Charlwood, thank you,' she returned with arrogance. 'I've often stayed with your aunt there.'

'Of course,' he nodded acknowledgment of the fact. 'But I'm afraid that without me you might have a little trouble getting inside the gates today.'

As Brooke had said, she had visited Jocelyn at her private cottage half a mile away from the main house many times, and never once had any trouble passing through the guarded gates. She gave Rafe Charlwood a puzzled frown.

'Only the cars carrying the family are cleared through our security today,' he explained in a dry drawl, as the black limousines began to file slowly past them.

'I've often wondered why you need the security at all,' she derided, knowing that he had an extensive system set up throughout the grounds and house.

His mouth tightened. 'I'm a rich man,' he bit out. 'There have been too many kidnappings of members of wealthy families for me to take any risks with my son.'

Brooke didn't argue with him any further, but got in behind the wheel to open his door for him, turning on the ignition to follow the limousines. 'I've met your son several times—at Jocelyn's,' she explained lightly. 'Is there—really any possibility of someone wanting to harm him?' She gave Rafe Charlwood a sideways glance as she drive.

'Yes,' he rasped. 'And today would give them the ideal opportunity to make such a move, during the confusion of the funeral.'

He sounded very calm, considering it was his son he was discussing as being a possible kidnap victim. God, she thought, this man really was inhuman, every action and word only confirming it.

The security around the house was indeed tight; the electronic gates were also guarded by a man, and the man who greeted them at the door of the house also seemed to check on everyone who entered.

'Not that way,' Rafe instructed curtly as Brooke would have followed the rest of the family into the main lounge. Charlwood was tastefully and elegantly furnished, a great and lasting compliment to Edwardian architecture, the house being surrounded by the immediate grounds of twenty acres, although Brooke knew the actual estate stretched for thousands of acres, containing several small-holdings. All the Charlwood family lacked for this to be a stately home was the title, already having the picture gallery of portraits of famous ancestors, the priceless antiques and furnishings passed down from generation to generation, even managing to have that vital asset so many titled families didn't possess nowadays—money. 'Mr Gardner has decided to read the will in the library,' Rafe explained at her questioning look.

The library. Just the word conjured up the massive book-lined room; many of the titles there were first editions, although this was just another wealth the Charlwood family took for granted.

A strange silence fell over the room as Brooke

entered at Rafe's side, and her eyes widened as she saw that only Rosemary and Patrick were seated in the room with the man sitting behind the mahogany desk who Brooke assumed to be Mr Gardner. Were they the only four beneficiaries? It would seem so.

Rafe Charlwood's hand remained beneath her elbow as he took her across the room to introduce her to Reginald Gardner.

'Miss Adamson,' the elderly lawyer greeted distantly. 'Now that we are all here,' he cleared his throat noisily, 'I would like to proceed with the reading of the will. There are—certain things I have to explain pertaining to its contents.' He seemed a little uncomfortable with the fact.

'I won't keep you much longer, Reginald,' Rafe Charlwood told him coolly, guiding Brooke over to the two waiting chairs. 'I believe you know my brother Patrick and his wife Rosemary,' he introduced casually as he saw her seated before lowering his weight into the armchair next to hers.

'Vaguely,' Rosemary snapped, her green eyes flashing her dislike, her short hair as black as the dress she wore with such style.

'I certainly do.' Patrick flirted with her, his blue eyes having an irrepressible humour even on such an occasion, his over-long hair a sandy blond, his easygoing nature no match for his wife's sharp tongue.

'Mr Charlwood, Mrs Charlwood,' Brooke greeted them both with cool indifference.

The lawyer cleared his throat once again, obviously deciding it was time they got on with the business in hand. 'Miss Charlwood was a very good friend of mine,' he began. 'I shall miss her a great deal.'

'I'm sure we all will,' Rafe snapped impatiently.

'Yes, yes.' The man placed horn-rimmed glasses on the end of his long nose. 'The will is quite a lengthy one, so I will just read out the relevant facts.' He shuffled

some papers about in his briefcase, taking out the
relevant ones and placing them tidily on the desk-top
before looking up at them. 'Not all the benefactors are
in this room,' he informed them nervously. 'But I have
done this for a reason——'

'I hope it's a good one,' Rafe Charlwood bit out
tautly.

'Indeed,' the older man was beginning to look
flustered. 'The people not here today receive only
nominal bequests, and the nature of the rest of the will
is rather—private, to the family,' he chose his words
with care.

Brooke sensed Rafe Charlwood stiffen at her side,
seeing the look that passed between him and Patrick
before his narrow-eyed gaze was turned on her. She felt
the colour move slowly up into her cheeks—almost as if
she were actually guilty of something!

'In that case you'd better proceed,' the head of the
Charlwood family instructed haughtily.

Reginald Gardner shot Rafe a nervous look and
shuffled the papers about even more. 'I—Yes, well, I—
I'll omit all the legal bumf and get straight to the point,
shall I?'

'I think that would be best,' the other man drawled
icily.

Brooke's hands clenched together tensely in her lap
as the lawyer began to talk, having a feeling, by the way
the lawyer had decided on secrecy for the reading of the
will to the family, that by the end of this meeting she
was going to be even more unpopular with them than
when she had arrived. What had Jocelyn *done*?

She listened as Reginald Gardner told them that all
Jocelyn's money went back to the family, relieved that
Jocelyn had kept her word about that. And yet she
could feel her tension rising with each modulated word
the man spoke, sensing that the 'private matter to the
family' was going to be a bombshell, and she was going

to be at the centre of it. She could tell the Charlwoods expected it too; Rosemary and Patrick were looking anxious, although Rafe's expression remained bland, as if he was prepared for whatever came next.

Reginald Gardner was starting to look flustered again, and Brooke felt her palms actually become damp. Oh, Jocelyn, what have you done? she cried silently.

'Now we come to Miss Charlwood's last bequest.' The lawyer shot Rafe another anxious look. 'I'm afraid it isn't straightforward, and——'

'For God's sake get on with it!' Rosemary snapped. 'All that's left are the shares Jocelyn had in the company.'

'And the cottage,' the lawyer reminded her softly.

'The cottage?' Rosemary frowned. 'But surely that reverts to the estate?'

'Not necessarily,' the lawyer shook his head. 'Mr Charlwood, your father,' he looked at the other two men in the room, 'and as such Jocelyn's brother, deeded both the cottage and its surrounding gardens to your aunt after the two of you were grown up and so no longer needed her at the main house.'

'But surely it was only for her lifetime?' Patrick spoke for the first time.

Reginald Gardner shook his head. 'There was no mention of that in the deeds.'

'But surely it was intended,' Rosemary persisted sharply.

'Intent does not make it so,' the lawyer told her stiffly. 'I drew up the deeds to the cottage, and neither by word or deed did Mr Charlwood imply that that was to be the case.'

'Read the rest of the will, Reginald,' Rafe Charlwood told him harshly, his features looking as if etched from granite. 'We can argue the legalities of this later.'

'Oh, it's legal,' the other man said indignantly. 'I

drew the will up' myself. It's just a little—unorthodox, that's all.'

'And obviously involves Miss Adamson,' Rosemary shot her another look of intense dislike.

'It involves you all ultimately,' he informed them quietly. 'I'll read out the last bequest now, although as I've already said, it's perfectly legal. "To my dear friend Brooke Adamson, I leave the cottage in the grounds of Charlwood for the duration of her lifetime when it will revert to the estate——" '

'Impossible!'

'Did Aunt Joss have a brainstorm?' Patrick echoed his wife's outrage.

Brooke had no idea why they were so surprised; after hearing that the cottage belonged to Jocelyn she had expected as much. She had a feeling by Rafe Charlwood's silence that he too had suspected it. Well, none of them need worry; she had no intention of accepting the bequest.

'Go on, Reginald,' Rafe invited softly.

'There's more?' Patrick mocked.

'Quite a lot more,' the lawyer nodded. 'And I can assure you that Miss Charlwood's faculties were perfectly in order when she made this will,' he told the young man sternly.

'Sorry,' Patrick murmured almost guiltily.

'Hm.' Reginald Gardner had stopped looking nervous now, continuing to read. ' "And to my nephews, Rafe and Patrick, I leave my shares in Charlwood Industries, eleven per cent to Rafe, nine per cent to Patrick, giving them fifty-one and forty-nine percent respectively—on condition that they make no effort to prevent Brooke Adamson inhabiting the aforementioned cottage." '

'That's ridiculous——'

'And if we do "make an effort" to prevent Miss Adamson living in the cottage?' Rafe Charlwood coolly interrupted his sister-in-law, surprisingly calm.

'Then the shares revert to Miss Adamson,' the lawyer told him in the hushed room.

Brooke swallowed hard, sensing the antagonism building up around her. 'What if I don't want the cottage?' she asked softly, not looking at any of the family, not needing to know of their resentment. 'Give it back to the family?'

'Then the shares automatically become yours, and you will have the controlling interest in Charlwood Industries,' the lawyer told her gravely. 'I have a letter for you here from Jocelyn.' He stood up to walk over to her, handing her an envelope. 'I have no idea of the contents,' he told her gently. 'But I do know that she intended you to have the cottage and not the shares. But it will, of course, be your decision.'

Brooke stood up to rip open the envelope, moving slightly away from the family as she read the contents of the handwritten sheets, vaguely aware of Rosemary Charlwood's cutting comments to her husband about the outrage of the contents of the will, declaring they would fight it.

All the discontent around her faded into the background as Brooke read the letter, and all she could do was silently thank her friend once again. Even in her illness Jocelyn had thought of Brooke, imposing the conditions of her will so that Brooke might be with her son at last—with Robert, the son she had given Rafe three years ago.

CHAPTER TWO

No, there was no shame attached to loving your child so much that you would do anything, *be* anything to be with him. And the girl who had once loved Rafe so much, who had found his power awesome, his air of remoteness daunting, his coldness a little frightening—a fear that had eventually grown to such proportions that she came to dread the rare times he was at home, that girl had become a woman who had been prepared to do anything to see again the son he had denied her.

Injured in the accident that Rafe still believed had killed her, she had begged the doctor not to repair the damage to her face until she looked as good as new, but to find her a doctor who could make her look *completely* new. It was a process that had taken months, but the first time she had seen Rafe again just under a year ago she had been rewarded for the time and pain spent in hospital by the way he had looked straight through her, not a vestige of recognition in the flinty grey eyes for the wife he believed had betrayed him with another man.

Jocelyn had been her only ally, the only one who knew of Jacqui Charlwood's transformation to Brooke Adamson. And even to the end Jocelyn had remained loyal, knowing that with her death Brooke's one doorway to seeing Robert had been closed. The cottage on the Charlwood estate had just thrown it wide open again. Brooke hugged the letter to her, hardly able to believe Jocelyn's final generosity to her.

She could see the Charlwoods couldn't believe it either. Rosemary and Patrick were in accord for once as they both loudly voiced their displeasure to poor

Reginald Gardner. Only Rafe appeared calm as usual—but then she had never been able to tell what he was really thinking, not even on the day he had asked her to marry him—and certainly not on the day he told her he intended taking her beloved baby away from her for ever. That was the day she really began to hate Rafe in earnest, even more than she feared him—because she didn't doubt he could make good his threat. And he had. Jacqui Charlwood hadn't been allowed to see her son since that day. But Brooke Adamson had, and she would continue to do so—no matter what price she had to pay.

'Well, Miss Adamson,' Rafe had walked over to her side without her being aware of it, his expression mocking as she hastily refolded the letter and thrust both it and the envelope into her clutch-bag. 'And what is your decision going to be?' he drawled. 'It would seem the future of Charlwood Industries rests in your hands.'

Brooke looked at him as coolly as ever, having been hurt too much by this man already ever to be intimidated by him again—or ever to fall again for the magnetic charm she knew he could display when it suited him to. And it had suited him before only for as long as it took him to marry her; after that she had just become another Charlwood convenience, there to be used when needed. God, no wonder she had grown to fear him!

But none of her thoughts showed in her clear blue eyes as she met his gaze, her expression thoughtful. 'And the cottage?' she mocked.

He shrugged broad shoulders beneath the tailored dark suit. 'Is yours with my compliments.'

She glanced over pointedly to where Rosemary and Patrick were now arguing with each other, a much more common occurrence than their agreement, she remembered. 'They don't seem to feel the same way,' she slowly taunted, enjoying this moment of power. 'Could that be because if I take the cottage *you* become head of Charlwood Industries?'

'I've always been the head of Charlwood Industries,' he said hardly. 'And I doubt even Patrick would welcome a complete stranger into the company as a shareholder.'

She didn't even stiffen at his insulting tone; she had learnt to school both her reactions and features as the latter had been slowly changed. 'But you don't mind inviting one to share your home?' she lightly mocked.

'The cottage is hardly my home,' he derided.

'But the Charlwood estate is,' she pointed out with coy sweetness.

'If my being here bothers you I can always arrange to live at one of our other houses,' he dismissed.

'I think perhaps,' she softly taunted, 'my being at the cottage would bother *you* rather than the other way around.'

Hard grey eyes raked over her with slow disdain. 'Believe me, Miss Adamson, where you choose to live is completely immaterial to me.'

'Really?' Dark blonde brows rose. 'In that case, I'd better give all this very serious thought. As you don't seem to care one way or the other——'

'I didn't say that, Miss Adamson,' he bit out, evidence that he wasn't quite as controlled as he appeared, although his eyes were glacial, his mouth the forbidding line she remembered so well. 'I would, of course, prefer the Charlwood shares to remain in the family.'

In that case she could decide on either of the conditions in the will, because if she did take the shares they would simply revert to Robert on her death. But she already knew that she was going to live in the cottage, could hardly contain her relief and elation at the thought of still being able to catch the occasional glimpse of the son who had been taken from her when he was only six months old. He had been a beautiful baby, and had grown up into a lovely little boy, but his babyhood had been robbed from her by the man standing at her side. She would never hear Robert call her 'Mummy' either, and all because this man had ruled her fate by his moral judgments on her, deciding she was unfit to be the mother of his child. She was no more unfit to be his mother than Rafe was to be his father!

'I understand that,' she told him coldly.

'But you still need time to think about your decision?' he rasped.

'Yes,' Brooke nodded, knowing it was time to cut short this private conversation with this potentially dangerous man. 'And now if you don't mind, I would like to leave.' She raised her voice enough to encompass the rest of the people in the room, her gaze remaining unflinching in the face of the hostility that surrounded her.

'You'll contact me when you've made your decision, Miss Adamson,' the lawyer asked politely; he was the only one who wasn't antagonistic, although he did seemed slightly puzzled by it all.

'Of course.' She moved to shake his hand, nodding coolly to the married couple before turning to leave.

'I'll walk you to the door.' Rafe fell into step beside her.

She gave a cool nod of acceptance and moved with graceful elegance at his side.

'I've spent some time with my son, Miss Adamson,' he suddenly drawled, 'so I'll now repeat my dinner invitation to you.'

She turned to look at him as they reached the door. 'And I'll repeat my refusal,' she said without emotion. 'No, thank you.'

His gaze was rapier-sharp as it raked over the

beautiful perfection of her face. 'Besides the fact that
you disapprove of the way I'm bringing up my son,' he
drawled, 'what else have I done to make you dislike
me?'

She arched shaped brows. 'Isn't that enough?' she
asked disdainfully.

His mouth twisted, his confidence now wavering for a
moment. 'Do you come from a broken home yourself?'

'Both my parents are dead, yes.'

'Ah.'

Brooke drew in a deep breath at his patronising tone.
'They died when I was a child, I never really knew
them. I just believe that any parent should bring up
their child themselves if they're able to, and not leave it
to servants.' She could see that this time she had got
beneath the coolness of his guard, his mouth tightening
ominously at her rebuke.

'Someone should have mentioned that fact to my
wife,' he bit out contemptuously.

She forced herself not to react as bitterly to that
derogatory remark as she was tempted to do. She had
suffered too much to get this far, she wasn't going to
lose all that for the satisfaction of wiping the arrogance
off Rafe's face for just a few minutes—that was as long
as it would take him to recover from the fact that his
wife wasn't dead after all, and to have her thrown out
of his home as quickly as possible. No, even that
satisfaction wasn't worth giving up the chance to be
with her son.

She met his contempt with some of her own. 'I
believe I said if they are able to, Mr Charlwood,' she
drawled dismissively.

'Meaning?' His voice had lowered threateningly.

'Meaning your wife wasn't given the chance to bring
up her child. You brought in a nanny from the day
your son was brought home from the hospital, engaged
a nurserymaid to help her out with his care. I wouldn't

say that left a lot of time for your wife to be involved in bringing him up, would you? Except perhaps for an hour or so before dinner?' Her voice was heavily laced with sarcasm.

'You would seem to know a lot about my marriage, Miss Adamson,' Rafe grated.

She didn't just know about it, she had *lived* it! From the moment Robert had been placed in her arms after his birth she had loved him, but Rafe had insisted she couldn't take care of him herself, that it would tire her too much. After that she hadn't seen enough of Robert for him even to become familiar of her as his mother, the army of servants Rafe employed for his son's care making it obvious that he believed her incapable of looking after him properly. And then he had wondered why she became bored and dissatisfied with her life at Charlwood!

'As you once mentioned, Mr Charlwood, your separation was much—publicised,' she derided. 'I believe at the time we were allowed to hear your wife's side of the marriage too.'

'A side with which you obviously sympathise,' he bit out.

She straightened her slender shoulders. 'Any woman would feel compassion for another woman who was so callously denied her child.'

'Callously, Miss Adamson?' he repeated savagely, his nostrils flaring angrily, his eyes like chips of ice as he looked down at her. 'You don't know the first thing about my marriage.'

'Perhaps not,' she agreed lightly. 'Maybe you would care to enlighten me some time?'

'I doubt it,' he told her glacially. 'I don't discuss it with anyone.'

Brooke nodded with cool dismissal. 'I'll be in touch with Mr Gardner concerning the will.' She looked pointedly at the door, waiting for him to open it before leaving with a haughty confidence she maintained until she had unlocked her car and driven down the driveway, raising her hand in only a polite token of acknowledgment to the man who stood so rigidly proud at the top of the stone steps that led into the house.

He looked very like the first time she had ever seen him in that moment, so darkly arrogant, so commanding, so *handsome*. Before setting eyes on Rafe Charlwood she hadn't believed such men existed outside of the pages of books or up on the big screen. He had been everything she believed tall, dark, and handsome should be and never hoped to find, had an experience and air of power that had merely added to his already devastating attraction.

Brought up by an aunt and uncle who had little interest in her, having no desire for children of their own, let alone an orphaned niece, she had been overjoyed when she won a scholarship to one of the famous schools for dance, and was happy there for the first time in years, despite being told that although she had the height and build of a ballet dancer she would never have that elusive talent that would make her into a star, the tutors advising her to concentrate on modern dance. It had been something she enjoyed more than anything else, teaming up with five other girls from the school to do a round of auditions that seemed never-ending, and rarely successful. But after almost a year together, and a change in a couple of the girls, they had finally managed to secure a season with Greg Davieson on his own television show. It had been like the realisation of a dream, the glamorous parties they were invited to being just a bonus as far as she was concerned.

And then at one of those after-the-shows parties she had seen Rafe. He had been talking with the producer and director, and she learnt from one of the other girls that he was a friend of the former, was the powerful owner of Charlwood Industries. He was a man often in the news for one business merger or another, and at thirty-five he looked his age—and he was also the most handsome and most sought-after man in London at the moment. Jacqui felt sure she didn't have a chance with him, wished she had worn something a little more mature, more sophisticated. She had come straight to the party from the show, just wanting to relax a little. The dress she had changed into was a simple yellow jersey, the colour clashing abominably with her red hair. With a natural colour of mousy-brown, and two blondes already in the group, she had decided on a more interesting shade of auburn. At their first conversation Rafe had told her he much preferred redheads to blondes, and from that moment on she had decided to keep her hair auburn.

Greg Davieson had introduced them, and to Jacqui's surprise they had spent the remainder of the evening together. When the party broke up at two o'clock in the morning Rafe Charlwood had been the one to drive her home, *his* home, his apartment in London. For two more weeks they had been together constantly. Jacqui was as yet unsure of Rafe's feelings for her, no closer to knowing the inner thoughts of this man than she had been before she spoke to him, and yet knowing that she was in love with him. She had known it that first night, had given him her innocence without thought of denial, and didn't hesitate on any occasion after that when he telephoned her and wanted to be with her. The night he had asked her to marry him she had been sure he loved her, although he still didn't say the words, not even at the height of passion, but remained a very private and insular man.

Her life had changed irrevocably the moment she became Rafe's wife—that much she had realised when a whole new wardrobe of clothes had been packed for her in the expensive suitcases they took with them on their honeymoon, her own clothes dismissed by Rafe as unsuitable attire for his wife. She had accepted the change of clothes, although the new ones hadn't really been the style she liked to wear, being smart rather than modern, elegant rather than stylish. But she had been too much in love with the strong man who was her husband to care about the subtle changes he made in her life, and she was overjoyed when he told her only a month after their wedding that he would like her to have his child. She had been ecstatic eight weeks later when she could tell him he was to have his wish. But it was then that even more changes began to happen in her life—the termination of her dancing career by Rafe as soon as he knew she was carrying his child, the way meetings with friends from her past life as a dancer became rarer and rarer, her life at the Charlwood estate becoming almost unbearable as her pregnancy became advanced, and Rafe forbade her to exert herself in any way. He spent more and more time away on business, and she had to contend with Rosemary's bitter jealousy over her pregnancy when she couldn't have children of her own.

As her pregnancy neared its latter months she saw even less of Rafe, not even having him close to her at night, as he no longer made the trips from his adjoining bedroom to hers, her enlarged condition making it impossible for them even to make love any more. Without that closeness between them any more she became more and more uncertain of herself, feeling the difference in their backgrounds and ages in a way she never had before. She began going up to London to see her old friends.

The first time she lied about seeing the girls she used to dance with she knew she had made a mistake, but she hated it when Rafe became angry or disapproving, and came to dread those times when she had to listen to him lecturing her on maintaining her position as his wife and the mother of his expected child.

Her visits to the rehearsals of the show, with her replacement going through the routines with the other five girls, became increasingly frequent, and the lies to Rafe along with them, the excuses becoming easier to make as time went on. But she was sure that with the birth of their baby everything would come right between them again.

It had been worse. Robert had been taken over by servants as soon as they returned home, so much so that Jacqui felt superfluous, to both him and Rafe. When she asked him if it would be possible for her to begin working again now that the baby was born and he was being taken care of so well Rafe had almost exploded with anger, telling her that if he had wanted a 'damned showgirl' he would have taken himself a mistress, not a wife, that it was time she settled down and realised her position as his wife. His last instruction at the end of that argument had been that she wasn't to see or visit the girls at the television studio ever again.

And for several months she had obeyed him, although it hadn't been without resentment. Rafe's punishment for that had been once again to stop sharing her bed, treating her with a coldness that had made her cry herself to sleep on more than one occasion, her sister-in-law's barbs about her lack of ability to hold her husband's attention past the first wedding anniversary rubbing salt into an already open wound.

It had been after one of these more than bitchy exchanges with Rosemary that Jacqui had left the estate with a defiance that had sent her to the studio, to an agreement to take the place of one of the girls in the dance group after she fell during rehearsals and twisted her ankle. It had been an impetuous and rebellious act on her part, since the programme was being televised later that evening. After such a defiant gesture on her part it had seemed stupid not to go to the after-the-show party, deciding that Rafe might as well chastise her for really disobeying him. She hadn't expected him to come to the party, to take one look at her laughing and flirting lightly with Greg, and have her locked out of the estate.

The guard on the gate told her he had instructions not to let her into the grounds, and even her impassioned telephone call to Rafe had met with chilling uninterest. He had told her she would be hearing from his lawyers!

She had heard from them; she could hardly believe that Rafe meant them to separate and keep Robert himself just because he had seen her at a party with Greg. But Rafe had refused even to talk to her, all his contact being made through his lawyers. Those lawyers had been paid well to produce evidence of her affair with Greg Davieson—and produce it they had, each visit to her friends at the television studio being made to look as if it were a personal one to Greg, the nanny and nurserymaid engaged to look after Robert making it look as if she had no interest in her child. How she had fought against that—but her defence of herself had been weak. Rafe had got his separation, had got his son too, and Jacqui had been awarded a large settlement and told she could see her son when it was convenient to Rafe.

It was never convenient to him. After five months of trying to see Robert she was ready to have a nervous breakdown. She hadn't managed to see her son or Rafe since the legal separation.

With Rafe's influence the Greg Davieson show had been cancelled, and both he and the girls, Sensuous Romance, had been out of a job, with no possibility of getting another one when it was known Rafe Charlwood didn't want them to. Sensuous Romance had decided to try their luck in America, and they had invited Jacqui to go along with them. She was almost past caring what she did by then, knowing that Rafe would stop her seeing Robert at any price. Her efforts to take him to court for access to her son had been in her favour, yet still he defied those orders. She had appealed to his aunt then. Jocelyn was always her ally, and had agreed to bring Robert to see her. But Rafe had found out about that too, and had warned her, through his lawyers once again, that if she did anything like it again he would have her charged with kidnapping. At that moment she had known that Rafe was too powerful and cruel an adversary for her to fight and win, and the decision to go to America was taken out of her hands.

The car crash so soon after their arrival in Los Angeles had left three of the six girls dead, the others seriously injured. Jocelyn Charlwood had been the one to come over to America to identify the body of her niece-in-law, only to find that she was still very much alive, although her head injuries meant that she could be scarred for life. Jocelyn had wanted to tell Rafe that his wife was still alive, but Jacqui's pleading that she didn't, the fact that the doctor warned that she was on the verge of a complete nervous breakdown, had persuaded Jocelyn not to do so. For three days and nights the older woman had sat by her bedside, had talked her back to sanity, had promised to help in any way she could, and had agreed to help her see Robert after the plastic surgery had been completed.

And she had. She was still helping even now she was dead, knowing that the cottage was the only way Jacqui—or Brooke as she was now called—could ever be with her son. Rafe's hatred of her was so deep that he would never let her near Robert if he once guessed who she really was.

She should never have become Rafe's wife, she knew that now. It would have been so much better, for them all, if Rafe *had* just kept her as his mistress. But then she wouldn't have given him his son, and that had been what he married her for, after all; she had learnt the truth of that from her last heated exchange with Rosemary. Rafe had never loved her, didn't want to get married at all, but with Rosemary's barren state a Charlwood heir was needed, and it was up to him to provide it. A nice unobtrusive wife who could give him a son and then be dismissed from his life had been the reason he married her.

With only an uncaring aunt and uncle for a family she must have seemed the perfect choice to him, a little nobody who pleased him in bed—for a time. Her boredom, her defiance in seeing Greg Davieson and her old friends, must have greatly annoyed him, especially the scandal that had been caused, and reported in the newspapers, when she had fought him for custody of their child. Her death so soon after their separation must have seemed providential to him, having meant the scandal wasn't raked up again when he actually divorced her. The fact that he hadn't even come to Los Angeles to identify the body himself just proved that he had never cared for her.

Charlwood looked more imposing than normal as she drove up to the gates three weeks later, expecting an argument with the guard, prepared to meet it with one of her own. To her surprise the gates swung open as soon as she approached them in the Porsche, and the man waved her through with a friendly smile.

How ironic, she thought. She wouldn't have got within a mile of the house if it were known who she really was, and yet here she was driving straight past the main house, her cottage being about half a mile away, far enough away for her to live in privacy, but near enough for her to catch the occasional glimpse of Robert. He was a very healthy little boy, very robust she just hoped that his father didn't break his spirit as he had once broken hers.

She had seen nothing of Rafe during the last three weeks, although she knew he had been informed by the lawyer of her decision to accept the cottage and not the shares. The lawyer had seemed relieved by her decision when she called him several days after the funeral. Her own feelings were still mixed—relief at being able to see Robert, dread at the thought that she would also see Rafe. Whatever love she had once felt for him had been slowly destroyed during their year of marriage, his savage taking of Robert from her making her hate him. And it was that hatred that she feared. At the moment Rafe seemed to be lightly pursuing her, the dinner invitations very real. But if he became too persistent, as she knew he could be, she was frightened what she might say to him in anger. Because she would never consent to going out with him, knowing too well the brand of pain he inflicted.

Jocelyn's cottage—she doubted she would ever be able to think of it as anything else!—faced away from the main house towards the river, its setting beautiful among the old oak trees, surrounded by a small neatly kept garden, wild roses trailing up and along the walls in a kaleidoscope of colour.

It was beautifully peaceful, far removed from the formality of the main house. Jocelyn had lived alone here until the last few months before her death, when Rafe had insisted she have one of the maids from the house to do the cleaning and cooking. Brooke had decided she would remain here alone herself, so the maid was back in the main house now, her own days being long and empty enough for her to take care of herself. After the accident, in which one of her legs had been broken and retained a weakness, dancing had been out for her, and with the money she had left from Rafe's more than generous settlement on her after the separation, she had no need to work anyway, aware that if she did she would stand little chance of seeing Robert. Rafe had never placed a lot of importance on money—probably because he had so much of it!—and as far as she knew he had never enquired what had happened to her fortune after her death. As far as she was aware he hadn't given her a second thought after that!

The cottage was as charming inside as it was out, olde-worlde, with chintzy furniture and curtains. Brooke felt as if she had come home after a long time away, and she put down her suitcases to look about her appreciatively, sure that she was going to be happy here.

Although the vase of yellow roses on the coffee-table struck a note of unease, and she walked over to read the card tucked among the blooms, dropping it again as if it had burnt her as she read the message written there. 'Welcome to Charlwood, Rafe'. The message differed in only one word from the one that had accompanied the red roses that had been placed in her bedroom when she came back to Charlwood a new bride, but then Rafe had added 'love' before his name. The emotion had proved to be as false as the man himself, and taking the vase of yellow roses she threw them into the bin in the kitchen, feeling no remorse for the perfect yellow blooms, the fragments of the ripped card scattered on top of them.

'Hello?'

She turned sharply at the sound of that soft query, leaning back against the unit as she saw her son standing at the doorway he had quietly opened. Pain stabbed at her heart that she couldn't pick him up and hold him the way she wanted to, but she knew that would only distress him—their acquaintance had so far been casual in the extreme. Although she intended changing all that, and as soon as possible.

'Hello, Robert,' she greeted lightly, closing the cupboard door firmly on the discarded roses. 'You know who I am, don't you?' she prompted gently as he still looked a little uncertain of her, his eyes as blue as her own, the only feature he had inherited from her as far as she could tell, the rest of him being all Rafe. But at least he didn't have those cold grey eyes.

'Brooke,' he nodded shyly. 'You visit Aunt Jossy sometimes.' He frowned suddenly. 'She's gone away, you know,' he spoke with a maturity far beyond his three years. 'Nanny Perkins says Aunt Jossy has gone to see God, but Connie says she's dead. What's dead mean?' he frowned his puzzlement.

Brooke knew that Maureen Perkins, a woman of fifty, looked after Robert in the position of nanny, and that Connie Roberts, a girl of twenty, helped out in the nursery. They had both been waiting at the house the day she brought Robert home, and although her dislike of them wasn't personal she still couldn't bring herself to like or accept the fact that two other women were bringing up her son.

'It means that that person has gone away,' she explained gently, 'and that they will never come back.'

His still-babyish face creased into a frown of concentration. 'Does that mean my mummy is dead?' he asked, his shyness evaporating quickly as curiosity took over.

Her breath caught in her throat. She didn't want to lie to her child, would give anything to be able to tell him she was alive and that she loved him very much. But she was under no illusions, knowing that Rafe would never allow her to be Robert's mother, that if he even guessed who she was he would once again take Robert away from her.

'She went away,' Robert continued when she hadn't answered him. 'Daddy said for ever. So does that mean she's dead?'

'I suppose it must do,' she evaded.

'Oh,' he looked disappointed by her answer. 'Other children have mummies, don't they?'

'Yes,' she nodded.

'And they don't go away?'

She swallowed hard, never guessing that her first conversation with him would be about such a subject! 'Sometimes they do.'

'But not always?'

She went down on her haunches so that she was on a level with him, although he made no move to come to her. She knew from past visits here that Robert was a reserved little boy when it came to giving affection, that Jocelyn had been the only one he ran to unreservedly. He was going to miss his great-aunt very much, and with that natural affection now gone Robert could very soon be as removed from emotion as his father was. It was a grim prospect to imagine in such a beautiful little boy.

'Mummies can't always help it when they go away,' she soothed. 'My own mummy went away, and I'm sure she didn't want to.'

'Aunt Rosemary says that Mummy didn't want me,' he announced calmly. 'That she didn't want to live with Daddy and me,' he explained. 'Nanny Perkins says Mummy didn't want to live with Daddy and me once I was borned.'

'Born,' Brooke corrected dazedly, wondering how Rosemary could have been so cruel to a little child.

'Yes,' he nodded. 'She was talking to Daddy, and I listened. They were talking about me——' he looked puzzled for a moment, then he shrugged it off with the casualness of the very young. 'Aunt Rosemary said my mummy was prom—promi——' he looked chagrined that he couldn't say the word.

Brooke was ashen, knowing exactly what Rosemary had accused her of being, and she had had no right to do so in front of Robert. 'You shouldn't listen to other people's conversations, Robert!' Her voice was sharper than she intended, and she hated the way he looked upset by the rebuke. 'Would you like some lemonade?' she offered lightly. 'I have some in the back of my car.'

'The green one outside?'

'Yes,' she nodded encouragingly.

He seemed to hesitate, and then he nodded. 'I like lemonade.'

'Good.' She stood up, holding out her hand to him, her breath catching in her throat as he trustingly put his little hand into hers. At least he hadn't yet learnt to distrust everyone as his father had.

She was furiously angry about what little information Robert seemed to have acquired about his mother. Not only had she not wanted him or his father, she was also promiscuous! Robert might be too young to know the meaning of that word yet, but one day he would, and then he would despise her. Rosemary had no right to say such a thing about her in front of the intelligent and observant child Robert obviously was. Especially as it wasn't true.

Robert helped her carry in some of the groceries from the car, the bottle of lemonade and the packet of chocolate biscuits being his main interest!

Brooke found it a little disconcerting to be sitting down at the kitchen table with her son like this; she hadn't expected to see him so soon after her arrival. Not that she was complaining; she would have him here all day every day if she could. But after he had been at the cottage for over an hour, devoured six chocolate biscuits and drunk two glasses of lemonade, she began to wonder if perhaps it wasn't time he went back to the main house. It was getting quite late.

'Robert,' she voiced slowly, 'won't Nanny Perkins and Connie wonder where you are?'

He looked up at her with clear blue eyes, somehow

seeming lost on the kitchen chair that was too big for him. 'Probably,' he nodded unconcernedly.

'Your daddy too?' she queried tentatively.

'Daddy's at work,' he dismissed unhesitantly. 'Could I have some more lemonade, please?' He looked at her with candid blue eyes.

Brooke desperately wanted to be his friend, was probably over-anxious to be that, and giving in to him over a third glass of lemonade wasn't a good idea. Besides the fact that she thought he had already had enough, no one at the Charlwood household would thank her if Robert were up all night with a stomach-ache because of her. In fact, he would probably be banned from coming here again if that happened.

She shook her head regretfully. 'I think you should be getting back now. I don't want——'

Before she could say any more the kitchen door burst open without warning, a furious-looking Rafe standing in the doorway, his ruggedly handsome face twisted with anger. 'Get back to the house, Robert,' he bit out coldly as his son would have gone to him.

The little boy looked up at his father uncertainly, the evidence of the chocolate biscuits he had consumed since his arrival still about his mouth.

Brooke could have cried for him, at the almost hero-worship that had disappeared from the excited blue eyes as soon as his father raised his voice to him. It was obvious from his reaction that Robert loved his father very much.

'Robert!' Rafe rasped in a controlled voice as the little boy still stood dumbstruck in front of him, not understanding why he was being shouted at in this way.

And neither did Brooke! What on earth was wrong with the man, couldn't he see he was frightening his own child? 'Let's get your hands and face washed first, Robert,' she suggested gently. 'Then you'd better do as your daddy says and go back to the house.'

Robert didn't say a word as she helped him stand on the chair to wash his face and hands, and neither did the rigidly controlled man standing across the room from them, although his presence was impossible to ignore, even for a few seconds; the anger emanating from him was a tangible thing. So much for his welcome!

At last Robert was as clean as when he had arrived, only a smudge of chocolate on his blue tee-shirt and a small wet patch of lemonade on his jeans telling of the feast he had eaten in her kitchen.

'Thank you very much,' he said gravely before walking to the door and looking up ruefully at his father. 'Goodbye, Daddy.'

His father gave a cold inclination of his head, holding the door open pointedly. The little boy went through it, and the door closed decisively behind him as Rafe turned glacial eyes back to Brooke.

She drew in a deep controlling breath at the censure she saw in his gaze, wanting nothing more than to tell this man what she thought of his barbaric treatment of his son, what she thought of the way he had burst into her home like this. But before she could say anything he was the one who began to talk.

'Are you completely stupid, Miss Adamson?' he rasped. 'Or just insensitive?'

'I——'

'Do you have any idea of the worry you've caused by the thoughtless way you invited Robert in here?' He didn't give her the opportunity to answer his first accusations, let alone this third one. 'Do you realise that I have several of my employees searching the grounds for him right now? Of course you don't,' he dismissed coldly. 'Why should it bother you that I imagined some harm had come to my son?' he derided harshly. 'What do you know about being a parent!'

Brooke blanched at the injustice of this last

accusation, aware that it was this man who had robbed her of the opportunity of ever knowing the joys of motherhood. 'I could ask you the same thing!' Her eyes flashed deeply blue. 'The way you spoke to your son just now did nothing but induce fear in him!'

His mouth was a thin angry line, his body tense beneath the tailored brown suit and cream shirt he wore. 'It was meant to,' he stated icily. 'Robert knows he shouldn't wander off without telling anyone where he's going. And you should have had more sense than to encourage him! My aunt's will may have been conclusive, Miss Adamson,' he added with cold calm, 'but if you ever do anything like this again I will make it my business—my *pleasure*, to break it. Do you understand?'

Only too well. If her presence here caused too much friction Rafe meant to have her off the estate. And she had no doubt he could do it too!

'I see that you do,' he mocked her pale face, then he strode forcefully back to the door. 'Good day to you, Miss Adamson.' The door closed behind him with quiet violence.

Brooke sat down shakily on to a kitchen chair once she was sure he had gone. Heavens, she had only been at the cottage a couple of hours and already she and Rafe were at each other's throats! But she had seen Robert too, had spent time with him, and that was worth anything Rafe might do or say to her.

CHAPTER THREE

BROOKE had taken her cases upstairs and partially unpacked them when she heard a knock sound on the front door. For an unwanted guest in a little cottage on a private estate she was certainly receiving a lot of visitors! Maybe it was Rafe coming back to reiterate how stupid he thought she had been?

Connie Roberts stood outside the door, little changed in the last three years, small and pretty, with bright red hair and rather calculating brown eyes. With little difference in their ages, and the obvious unhappiness of her marriage, Brooke had often had difficulty in convincing this young girl in the past that she was mistress of Charlwood. Three years had made a lot of difference to Brooke's own self-confidence, although Connie still seemed to be as insolent.

'I'm sorry to trouble you,' she said with obvious insincerity. 'But have you seen Robert?'

Brooke looked at the other woman with unflinching blue eyes, wondering why she had let her, and the other employees at the main house, bother her in the past. The answer was obvious, of course; she had been too young and inexperienced in the Charlwood way of life to be able to handle her role as Rafe's wife with any confidence. And everyone there, including Rafe, had been aware of that.

But if Jacqui Charlwood had lacked confidence in herself Brooke Adamson did not, and she answered the younger woman coolly. 'Mr Charlwood has already taken Robert home,' she dismissed.

'Oh,' Connie looked surprised. 'He was here, then?'

'For a short time, yes,' she confirmed distantly.

53

Connie looked at her speculatively, obviously aware
that the Charlwoods didn't welcome her presence here
in the cottage; the nurserymaid would never have acted
this way in front of a member of the family, or a friend
of theirs either. 'Was Mr Charlwood very angry?' she
asked with relish.

Brooke's mouth tightened. 'I wasn't aware of it,' she
avoided.

Connie gave a knowing smile. 'We had to get him
back from London, you know,' she explained with
eagerness. 'Robert had been missing for about half an
hour, and we couldn't find him anywhere, so we called
Mr Charlwood and he came home immediately. He was
going to call in the police if we didn't find him in the
next hour,' she confided.

Now Brooke understood Rafe's blazing anger—he
thought Robert had been kidnapped! To be telephoned
and told that his son was missing must have been a
nightmare for him, to find the little boy sitting in *her*
kitchen calmly eating chocolate biscuits when he had
been imagining all sorts of horrors must have made him
furiously angry. Especially as she already knew of the
strict security surrounding Robert! Much as she
disliked—and dreaded—the idea, she knew she would
have to apologise to Rafe for her thoughtlessness. And
right now.

'Well, he's been found now,' she told the other
woman briskly. 'So if I were you I would get back to
the main house—otherwise they might send out a
search-party for you too!'

Connie bristled indignantly at being spoken down to
in this way. 'Perhaps if you decide to invite Robert over
in this way again you could let us know?' she said with
barely contained insolence.

Brooke met her gaze with steady blue eyes, not in the
least intimidated as she once would have been. 'I will
inform a member of the Charlwood family, yes,' she

replied with cool dignity. 'Now, if there was nothing else . . .?' she looked at the young woman with arrogant enquiry.

Connie became flushed with anger. 'Nothing at all,' she snapped.

'Then I'll say goodbye to you,' she said pointedly.

The girl looked even angrier, then turned away with a furious scowl, slamming the garden gate behind her.

The smile on Brooke's lips faded as soon as she closed the door; the prospect of talking to Rafe was not a pleasant one at all. There was always the possibility that her voice might sound familiar to him over the telephone—there were some things about a person you just couldn't change! Admittedly they had spoken on the telephone the day Jocelyn died, but she had been upset then, her voice lacking its usual husky tone. She would just have to make sure it was this time as well.

The telephone in the cottage had a direct line to the house, and she waited tensely for someone to answer her call.

'Mr Charlwood is not at home, Miss Adamson,' she was informed by the butler Shepherd when she requested to talk to Rafe.

'Rafe, not Patrick,' she explained.

'Yes, I understood, Miss Adamson,' she was told by the short, pleasantly plump man of indiscriminate years—although Brooke thought him to be in his early fifties. He had been with the Charlwood family for many years, she knew that. 'Neither Mr Charlwood or Mr Patrick are at home.'

'But——' she frowned her chagrin, 'Mr Charlwood was over here not half an hour ago.'

'Perhaps, Miss Adamson,' he acknowledged in his calming voice. 'But he went back to London several minutes ago.'

So much for his worry and concern over Robert—as usual Charlwood Industries came first with Rafe. She was surprised now that he had come home in the first place! 'Thank you,' she said stiltedly. 'I'm sorry I troubled you.'

'It was no trouble at all, Miss Adamson,' the butler returned smoothly. 'Mr Charlwood has instructed me to do anything I can to make things comfortable for you. I trust you had no trouble at the gates on your arrival?'

'None,' she answered stiltedly, having no doubt Rafe would have instructed the family to accept her here too. After all, it was better than having a 'complete stranger' owning any Charlwood shares!

'And you received Mr Charlwood's flowers?'

'Thank you—yes.' Her tone was even more clipped. As usual Rafe had instructed one of his employees to see to her comfort—she found it amazing that he had found the time to write the card that accompanied the roses himself!

'Could I give Mr Charlwood a message?' Shepherd asked politely.

'No, no message,' she told him dryly. 'Although you could tell me if Master Robert arrived home safely?' she added lightly, not wanting him to guess the importance she attached to his reply.

'Master Robert is in the nursery having his tea.' The man's voice warmed somewhat as he spoke of the youngest member of the Charlwood family.

Relief flooded through Brooke at his reply. She hadn't quite known what punishment she had expected Rafe to mete out to their son—a good spanking at least!—she certainly hadn't thought he would get off so lightly.

'Will that be all, Miss Adamson?' Shepherd cut into her thoughts.

'Er—yes. Thank you.' She rang off, remembering the first time she had met the rather proper and precise butler—Rafe had later reprimanded her for calling the other man *Mr* Shepherd, telling her the butler would consider it an insult to be addressed so formally by the mistress of the house. It had been only the first of many *faux pas* she had made as Rafe's wife.

She went slowly back up the stairs to finish off her unpacking. She had chosen to use the spare bedroom rather than the larger one that Jocelyn had always used. With his usual efficiency Rafe had had Jocelyn's personal things removed from the cottage, and the whole place had been given a spring-clean, and yet the bedroom next door would always remain Jocelyn's to her.

This bedroom was small and pretty, in cream and lemon, the lace curtains at the small Georgian window a delicate cream colour, as was the carpet and furniture, the quilt cover and wallpaper in a matching lemon and cream floral design. It was the room Brooke had always used when she visited in the past, and she felt comfortable in it.

She had sold all her own furniture with her flat in London, the modern style of design and colour not being suitable for this lovely little cottage. But she had brought a few of her more personal belongings, china ornaments and some paintings, and they added a homely touch. The cottage had many happy memories for her. It was here she had met her son again for the first time just under a year ago, the tiny baby with only two teeth and the ability to crawl small distances when encouraged having turned into a robust little boy of two years, the fine dark hair having grown to a riot of thick curls, his face still babyish, all his milk-teeth showing enchantingly when he smiled or giggled. Brooke had missed most of his babyhood, but at least she would see the rest of his growing up.

She didn't have a social life in London. She had remained without friends other than Jocelyn through necessity, never intending to become emotionally involved with another man. That might have seemed a strange and final decision for a woman of twenty-three to have made, but after her traumatic experience with Rafe she never wanted to fall in love again. But despite her lack of a social whirl previous to moving here she found the cottage very quiet, with only the sound of the river flowing nearby to break the stillness of the night, only the lights from the main house showing her she wasn't completely alone. No doubt she would get used to the peace and quiet here again in time.

Although it didn't seem all that peaceful and quiet at the moment—a knock had sounded on the cottage door! Brooke picked up the debris from the snack dinner she had prepared herself and carried it through to the kitchen, checking the respectability of her flowing housecoat, the zip reaching from the ground to her throat, the differing shades of blue suiting her blondness. Whoever her visitor was, and it had to be someone from the main house, they should have telephoned first if they wanted her to be prepared for their visit.

As soon as she opened the door she knew she should have checked out of the window first. Rafe stood outside, the light flowing out from the room behind her showing her he wore one of the dark evening suits that looked so good on him. Her own casual attire for eating her own dinner suddenly looked *too* casual!

She straightened her shoulders defensively. 'Mr Charlwood, it's late, and I——'

'I come bearing gifts.' He held up the bottle of wine in his hand.

Her eyes narrowed. 'There's a saying about that . . .'

Rafe's mouth quirked with amusement. 'I'm not Greek. Shepherd told me you telephoned the house this afternoon and asked to talk to me.'

She had forgotten all about that. 'I also told him I didn't want to leave a message.' She stood firmly in the doorway, determined he wasn't going to enter the cottage.

He gave a confident smile. 'The telephone call in itself was a message.'

Brooke frowned. 'It was?'

'Of course. That you wanted to talk to me.'

She flushed. 'That was then.'

'And now?' he quirked dark brows.

'Now it's late, I've had a long day, and I just want to go to bed.'

His steely gaze suddenly moved over her assessingly, seeming to know that she wore only a lace nightgown beneath the housecoat, lingering on her face that was pale in its bareness of make-up, seeming to frown as he met her blue-eyed gaze, puzzlement flickering briefly in the searching grey eyes.

Brooke could feel the panic rising within her. He couldn't possibly see young Jacqui Charlwood in sophisticated Brooke Adamson! And yet she was aware that at this moment she didn't look at all sophisticated, with her hair brushed loose from its feathered style, her lashes golden blonde, her face and mouth free of any make-up. And Rafe was starting to stare at her as if he had seen a ghost!

She gave a light laugh to break the moment. 'Perhaps one glass of wine.' She moved back to allow him access to the kitchen, doing her best to compose her features before turning to follow him as he strode arrogantly into the lounge.

Rafa turned to stare at her once again, and Brooke moved awkwardly to get two glasses out of the sideboard.

Finally she couldn't stand the tension between them any longer, and threw back her head to look him full in the face. 'Is there anything wrong?' she challenged.

His expression was harsh, his eyes narrowed. 'For a moment . . .'

'Yes?' she prompted hardly.

He turned away, picking up the corkscrew she had

put out for him to open the wine. 'For a few seconds you looked a little like—Jacqui,' he muttered as he bent over the bottle.

'Your wife?' she enquired lightly, her hands clenching into fists at her sides. What part of her could possibly belong to Jacqui; she had believed all of her long dead, along with the love she had once felt for this man! She was more slender now than ever before, her hair dark blonde instead of auburn, her features expertly changed; what could have reminded Rafe of his dead wife?

'Yes,' he bit out, looking at her again, his face suddenly haggard. 'It was your eyes,' he explained huskily. 'For a moment you looked at me as she used to.'

Brooke swallowed hard, knowing her eyes, like her voice, were something that couldn't be changed. But how had she looked at him, how could she have looked at him in a way that reminded him of the wife who had loved him unquestioningly?

He put the bottle and opener down with a clatter, turning his back on her to thrust his hands into his trouser pockets, his shoulders hunched over. 'You said this afternoon that I induced fear in Robert,' he spoke raggedly. '*She* used to fear me too,' he ground out, turning suddenly to face her, 'And just now *you* looked at me the same way.'

Relief made her laugh lightly dismissive. 'And why should I fear you, Mr Charlwood?'

'You tell me,' he bit out harshly.

'But I don't fear you at all,' she shrugged off the suggestion, moving to pour the wine herself as he seemed to show no inclination to do so. She needed something to steady her nerves! 'As you pointed out once before, it's difficult to dislike—or fear,' she added mockingly, 'someone you don't even know.'

He seemed to regain his control with an effort,

breathing deeply. 'Why did you telephone me this afternoon?' he rasped.

Brooke slowly sipped her wine, although Rafe ignored the glass she had poured for him. 'Connie came here after you'd left, and explained that you had to be called back from London to look for Robert. I had no idea I had caused such chaos by inviting him in here.'

'But you didn't,' he said dryly.

Her eyes widened. 'You had to come back from London, you had employees out looking for him——'

'I didn't mean that.' He at last moved to pick up his wine glass, drinking down the wine with little regard for its delicacy. 'You didn't invite Robert in, he invited himself,' he said grimly.

Brooke looked at him sharply, knowing by the way his mouth thinned and his eyes hardened that someone had earned his anger—and she had a feeling it had been Robert. 'Did he tell you that?' she asked slowly.

'Yes.'

'Before or after you punished him?'

He levelled cold grey eyes on her. 'After,' he bit out.

She swallowed hard, taking a large swallow of the wine, almost choking over it. 'And what form did his punishment take?' she asked steadily.

'He was to go on a drive to the park tomorrow, a particular favourite with him. He's no longer being allowed to go,' Rafe stated flatly.

Considering the fact that Robert had worried a lot of people with his disappearing act the punishment didn't seem too harsh to her. But she hadn't been blameless; she had been thoughtlessly selfish in keeping Robert here when she had guessed he should really go back to the main house. 'And what is my punishment to be?' she asked dryly.

He raised dark brows. 'Do you think you deserve one?'

'Probably,' she nodded. 'I encouraged Robert to stay here.'

'With chocolate biscuits and lemonade.' The austere features moved into an amused smile. 'He told me that too—after he was violently sick this evening,' he added softly.

'Oh, lord!' she groaned her consternation. 'That was my fault too!'

'Not exactly,' Rafe drawled, enjoying his wine now. 'He ate a big tea after leaving you. He was sure to be sick.'

'But if I hadn't——'

'It doesn't matter,' he dismissed arrogantly. 'The incident is over now.'

Brooke could see that it was too, at least as far as Rafe was concerned; she only hoped Robert would forget it as easily, and not blame her too much. 'Is he all right now?' she asked anxiously.

'He was tucked up in bed fast asleep when I looked in on him before coming over here.'

Brook looked at him curiously. 'Do you do that every night?'

He seemed to mentally withdraw from her, as if he deeply resented this questioning about his personal life. 'If I happen to be at home, yes,' he replied distantly, putting down his empty glass. 'I came here tonight to apologise for losing my temper with you earlier. It isn't something I usually do,' he added in a slightly puzzled voice.

'Does that mean you didn't really mean the threat you made about the cottage?'

He gave a deep sigh. 'Yes,' he bit out abruptly. 'Although I hope you'll have more sense than to encourage Robert to disobey my instructions again.'

She flushed at the rebuke, sensing that with her personal questions she had put them back on the footing of adversaries. 'But if I formally asked permission would you let him come over?' She didn't give a damn about her relationship with Rafe—in fact, she preferred them to be enemies!—but she didn't want to lose what could be a very close relationship with Robert.

'I'm sure you can't really want to be bothered with a small child——'

'On the contrary,' she contradicted tautly, 'I enjoyed having him here.'

Grey eyes narrowed on her with probing intensity. 'Do you have any children of your own?' he asked shrewdly.

Her blue gaze clashed with his, her face suddenly pale. 'What on earth makes you ask a thing like that?' she scorned lightly. 'If I had a child I would be with him.'

'Indeed?' Rafe rasped harshly. 'Not all women have such a maternal instinct.'

'If you're referring to your wife again, Mr Charlwood,' she defended heatedly, 'then I think——'

'I'm well aware of your opinion, Miss Adamson,' he interrupted lightly. 'And despite what the newspapers reported at the time, you can know nothing of the relationship between my wife and myself.'

'You admitted yourself a few minutes ago that she was frightened of you!'

His jaw tightened and his eyes blazed with fury. 'Goodnight, Miss Adamson,' he ground out, walking away from her. 'And once again, welcome to Charlwood!' His sarcasm barely contained his anger, the cottage door closing forcefully behind him a few seconds later.

Alienating Rafe in that way had been unwise, she knew that. If only he didn't keep criticising Jacqui at every turn! She couldn't control her anger when he did that, and she would have to if she were to get his permission to invite Robert over here, something he had omitted to give just now. After all this time she still had to get Rafe's permission to see her son!

*   *   *

She shouldn't have come here, she had known she shouldn't as soon as she arrived. The Charlwood 'get-togethers' had never been her idea of fun, with everyone standing around trying to outdo everyone else. This one, a wedding anniversary party for Patrick and Rosemary, was necessarily small in view of Jocelyn's death the month before, but there were still thirty or so people here.

Rosemary had come to the cottage personally and issued the invitation. Brooke had been dismayed when she opened the door to the other woman yesterday afternoon; she had been subjected to too many bitchy encounters with Rosemary in the past to view her with anything but suspicion. The invitation to this evening's dinner party had come as a complete surprise—although Rosemary had soon explained the reason for it.

'With you living so close it would look very odd if we didn't invite you,' she told Brooke haughtily, her keen green eyes looking critically about the lounge of the cottage. Only a few china ornaments and knick-knacks were different from when Jocelyn lived here, and Rosemary's interest was only fleeting. Those same green eyes raking over Brooke now, her mouth twisting contemptuously over the designer jeans and fitted blouse. Her own deep green suit was obviously made of silk, and suited her slender beauty.

The invitation was hardly a gracious one, only confirming the fact that Rafe had instructed everyone to accept Brooke's presence here, but after not having even a brief glimpse of Robert she was feeling desperate enough to accept. Rafe was away on business, she had learnt when she telephoned the house to speak to him three days ago, wanting to ask him if Robert might visit her, but he was expected back for the party this evening. She had thought the invitation for Robert to come and see her might be easier to make at a social gathering. And now Rafe wasn't even here—delayed on business, Rosemary had told her when she asked where he was.

Brooke could have screamed with the frustration of having to get through the rest of this evening until she could politely take her leave. Dinner had been bad enough, seated halfway down the long table, the men sitting either side of her curious about her connection with the Charlwood family, and more than interested when they learnt she was the unwanted owner of the Charlwood cottage. Another problem was that she had known both men when she was Rafe's wife, and had even had to repulse the advances of one of them at one time. And he had been no less the octopus tonight, continually touching her leg under the table. She would probably be bruised there tomorrow from fighting him off!

She had had the same glass of champagne in her hand for the last half hour since the toast had been made to Patrick and Rosemary, and the bubbles were falling a little flat now—as was her own spirit. She glanced at the slender watch on her wrist; a little before eleven, surely she could leave now?

'That's the third time you've looked at your watch in as many minutes,' remarked an amused voice. 'Are we boring you that much?'

She turned to face Patrick Charlwood, younger than Rafe at thirty-two, his nature as different from Rafe's as his looks were. Brooke had never been able to understand how such a charming man had got himself such a shrewish wife. The Charlwood brothers seemed to have been particularly unlucky in their choice of brides!

'I'm not bored,' she smiled at him, a natural smile; she had always liked Patrick. 'It's just that it's getting late and I'm tired.'

'And you have a headache. And then there's the cat to feed,' he mocked with raised brows, looking very attractive in his black evening suit and snowy white shirt.

She laughed softly. 'I don't have a cat.'

'No,' Patrick smiled acknowledgement of the fact. 'But you *were* starting to sound just a little desperate in your excuses to leave.'

'I'm sorry,' she shrugged. 'I just don't feel very sociable.'

He grimaced. 'To tell you the truth, neither do I, not at functions like this anyway. But Rosemary adores entertaining.' He took two glasses of fresh champagne from a passing maid, putting her old glass on the tray. 'And it's more peaceful around here when I indulge her,' he derided. 'Cheers,' he toasted her with the champagne, his gaze automatically moving to his wife as she laughed and talked with their guests. 'Yes, Rosemary loves all this,' a trace of bitterness entered his voice. 'It's what she married me for, after all.'

Brooke looked closely at the man at her side, seeing for the first time the lines of strain about his eyes and mouth, the effort he was having to make to keep up the appearance of enjoying himself. Patrick was not a happy man.

'Patrick——' she began.

'Is this a private conversation or can anyone join in?' drawled a harshly mocking voice.

The hand Brooke had placed on Patrick's arm slowly dropped away as she turned to face Rafe. He wore a similar dinner suit and shirt to his brother, and yet he wore it so much more elegantly than Patrick, looking stylish and darkly handsome. But his gaze was like ice as he saw the way she had been touching Patrick, and Brooke felt all the old unease she had always experienced when she happened to be pleasant to his brother in front of him. Rafe had always seemed to view any man his wife came into contact with as a possible lover for her, and they had had more than one argument over her friendship with Patrick. Although she was no longer his wife!

Patrick felt no inhibitions about welcoming his brother home, slapping him heartily on the shoulders. 'I thought you weren't going to make it.' His momentary strain of a few minutes ago disappeared as he grinned.

'I've never missed one of your anniversaries yet,' Rafe replied aloofly. 'I didn't expect to see you here, Miss Adamson.' Probing grey eyes were levelled over the top of his champagne glass as he sipped the bubbly wine.

'Nor I you.' She was at once on the defensive, as she always was with this man.

'I'll have to remember in future that you're always where I least expect to see you.' His gaze moved appreciatively over her body in the silver-blue weave dress that moulded to the slenderness of her body, then shifted back to her face, his eyes darkening in colour at how beautiful she looked tonight.

'I was just trying to persuade Brooke that we aren't all bores,' Patrick told him cheerfully, picking up none of the underlying tension between their politeness to each other.

'So I saw,' his brother drawled. 'Rosemary asked me to send you over to her.'

Patrick grimaced. 'I suppose I've got to be entertaining again. It was nice talking to you, Brooke,' he grinned at her. 'You brightened up what was otherwise a very dull party.'

There was a strained silence once Patrick had departed to join his wife, and Brooke was very much aware of the disapproval emanating from Rafe. What on earth did he think she had been doing—trying to seduce Patrick at his own wedding anniversary party? Knowing Rafe that was exactly what he did think; he didn't seem to think any woman had morals. But she was no longer Jacqui who had to beware of this man's anger, and if she wanted to have a perfectly harmless conversation with Patrick then she would. Rafe might not realise it, but his brother was far from a happy man, and Rosemary's gaiety was of the brittle kind that could break at any moment.

'So you find the party boring, Miss Adamson,' Rafe suddenly spoke to her.

Delicate colour highlighted her cheeks. 'Your brother was just teasing,' she dismissed. 'Although I was about to leave.'

'It's still early,' he raised dark brows.

'It's late for me.'

That silver gaze searched over her face for timeless minutes. 'I'll walk with you,' he said abruptly.

Brooke fluttered startled lashes. 'There's no need for that. It isn't far, and I'm not afraid of the dark.'

'Or me,' he reminded her mockingly.

'Or you.' Her eyes flashed.

Rafe's mouth twisted. 'Then you have no objection if I walk with you? I'm in need of the fresh air after being confined to offices and board-rooms for the last week.'

She didn't particularly want the company of this man, but she had yet to talk to him about allowing Robert to come and visit her at the cottage. 'By all means accompany me, Mr Charlwood.' She put down her empty glass, ready to leave now. 'How is Robert?' she asked to fill the silence as they went out into the hallway, having already made their excuses to Patrick and Rosemary, and the other woman's gaze was speculative as she realised Rafe was leaving with Brooke. 'I haven't seen him since you went away,' she added pointedly.

Rafe took her silver jacket from Shepherd and placed it about her shoulders himself, the lean strength of his

hands lightly brushing her arms. 'Then he took notice
of my instructions, didn't he?' he dismissed lightly.

'Yes,' she agreed, evading the sharpness of his gaze as
he moved to stand at her side.

'But you would rather he hadn't,' he guessed wryly.

'Not exactly,' she grimaced. 'I just—It's a little lonely
at the cottage.' Still she was loath to let him know how
desperately she wanted to see Robert.

'Surely there are bigger boys than Robert who would
just love to keep you company?'

She flushed at his mockery. 'It would be nice to see
Robert,' she said stubbornly.

Rafe looked down at her bent head with enigmatic
eyes. 'Do you really like children that much?' he asked
abruptly.

Brooke swallowed hard, unwilling to meet the
shrewdness of his gaze. 'Yes.'

Something flickered in the depths of his eyes,
something too fleeting to be defined. 'Would you like to
see Robert now?' he offered gruffly.

Her eyes widened to his, her breath catching in her
throat. 'Won't he be asleep?'

Rafe gave a humourless smile. 'Some people consider
that the best time of day as far as children are
concerned.'

Her mouth quirked at his dry humour. 'I'd love to
see him!'

Again Rafe seemed fascinated by the beauty of her face,
shaking his head as if to shut out the sight of her. 'Then
we'd better go upstairs, hadn't we?' he suggested softly.

Brooke allowed him to take her arm as they went up
the stairs together, hoping he couldn't detect the slight
trembling of her body at the contact. How many times
in the past she and Rafe had walked up these same
stairs together, usually to lose themselves in a transport
of ecstatic delight in each other's arms minutes later! It
was a disturbing thought.

'Cold?' Rafe murmured close to her ear.

'No—not really. Well, perhaps a little,' she amended awkwardly as she still trembled. 'That's the trouble with the English weather, you can never rely on it,' she referred to the last three days of rain; the weather being still cool even now.

'New York was hot, sticky—and unbearable,' Rafe drawled dismissively. 'I much prefer this.'

They had reached the nursery now. Brooke came to a halt outside the door, looking up at Rafe expectantly, hardly able to contain her excitement at the thought of seeing Robert again. It was even worth having Rafe's hand on her arm for this chance to see her son.

Then she realised her mistake—she shouldn't have known this was the nursery! She was a stranger to this house, or should have been.

'What a lovely transfer,' she laughed nervously as she looked admiringly at the gaily coloured aeroplanes on the door.

Rafe nodded abruptly, seeming to accept that this was how she had known it was his son's bedroom. 'Robert likes anything that can fly.' He moved closer to Brooke's side as he leant forward to open the door.

Brooke didn't even notice his proximity as they entered the room, her attention all on the tiny boy who looked so like his father as he lay asleep in the small single bed. The nursery itself was little changed; it was just as she had decorated it before Robert was born, although the toys on the floor and on the shelves were for an older child now. The cot had been replaced by a short single child's bed, the quilt cover was patterned with helicopters and aeroplanes.

'I told you,' Rafe derided softly as she smiled at the latter.

Brooke didn't respond, her throat was choked with emotion. Robert looked so young when he was asleep, thick dark lashes fanned out across his baby cheeks, a slight curve to the pouting mouth, his dark curls ruffled into disorder.

'Satisfied that I don't have him imprisoned in his room?' Rafe mocked huskily.

She turned stricken eyes up to his dark face, the only illumination in the room coming from a small night-light on the bedside table, a small aeroplane lit up from inside. 'I never thought——'

'Didn't you?' he taunted. 'You gave a different impression downstairs.'

She swallowed hard, then turned to leave as Robert moved restlessly in the bed, his eyes opening sleepily to focus on his father, a pleased smile transforming his features.

'Daddy!' His arms came up about his father's neck as he bent over him. 'You're back!'

Brooke watched in fascination as Rafe and Robert shared a moment of tenderness, Rafe gently kissing his son on the cheek before releasing his thin little arms from about his neck to tuck him firmly beneath the quilt, as the little boy fell back into a contented sleep. For those few brief moments Rafe had revealed his deep love for his son, a deep love that somehow made him seem all too human, a love that, if she hadn't seen it for herself, she would have sworn he could never feel for any child she had given him.

She followed him from the room, giving one last longing look at Robert before softly closing the door.

'Well, well, well,' drawled a mocking voice. 'I thought you two had left long ago.'

Brooke turned with a guilty start to face Rosemary Charlwood, although Rafe felt no such emotion, smiling easily at his sister-in-law, who was looking dazzling in a deep green dress.

'Just checking on Robert,' he dismissed.

'Really?' Cold green eyes were turned on Brooke. 'You like children, Miss Adamson?'

What was the matter with this family, wasn't a liking for children considered normal? 'Very much,' she answered stiltedly. 'Now I really must be going,' she said firmly.

Rafe took a proprietorial hold of her arm. 'We mustn't keep you from your own party, Rosemary.'

The other woman gave a tight smile. 'You must come to dinner again some time, Miss Adamson, when we can talk more intimately. I'm sure Patrick would like that,' she added bitchily.

Lean fingers bit into Brooke's arm, and it was Rafe who answered the taunt. 'I have a feeling I would like it more than Patrick,' he said lightly. 'I'll see you later, Rosemary,' he added by way of dismissal, as he guided Brooke down the stairs.

She hadn't realised how stiffly she was holding herself until she got outside the house, and heaved a shaky sigh as her tension was released.

'Yes,' Rafe sighed too. 'You've just learnt that my sister-in-law doesn't only have green eyes. She has a very possessive streak where Patrick is concerned.'

Brooke had a feeling the other woman's jealousy hadn't been completely on her husband's behalf, that the fact that Rafe was accompanying her back to the cottage might also have something to do with it; Rosemary had always had a possessive streak where *both* the Charlwood men were concerned!

But they were back at the cottage, thank goodness! Brooke turned as they reached the door, intending to say goodnight to him here. 'I mustn't keep you from the party any longer,' she thanked him lightly. 'Especially as you were late arriving.'

Rafe pushed the unlocked door open behind her, turning on the kitchen light to stride into the room, taking it for granted that Brooke would follow him as he went through to the lounge. She had no choice!

Rafe stood with his back to the unlit fireplace as she

entered the room, his face looking harsher than ever in the light of the single lamp he had turned on. 'I nearly didn't make the party at all,' he told her gruffly.

'Oh?' Brooke took off her jacket with a casualness she was far from feeling and put it down carefully on one of the high-backed chairs.

His mouth was taut. 'The work I had to do in New York took me twice as long as usual—and it was all your fault.'

She blinked golden-tipped lashes, moistening her lips nervously. 'My fault?' she echoed lightly. 'How on earth could that be true?'

'I couldn't concentrate.' He held her gaze easily with his. 'That's been happening a lot the last few months, but more so since you decided to move in here.'

She raised mocking brows. 'My presence here bothers you that much?'

'That much,' he nodded grimly.

'I can assure you I never meant it to,' she frowned. 'I would have thought you would prefer me to take this cottage rather than the shares, in fact you said as much to me the day of the funeral. I realise you would rather I'd never come here at all,' she mocked. 'But surely this is the lesser of two evils?' she taunted him.

His mouth twisted. 'You still don't understand, do you, Brooke?' he derided.

Her expression was apprehensive as she searched the harshness of his face. It gave nothing away, but then it never had. 'Understand what?' She wished she had been able to control that uncertain tremble in her voice, sure that he must have noticed it.

'How much I want you.'

CHAPTER FOUR

BROOKE'S expressive eyes widened with panic; she felt shivery and warm at one and the same time. Rafe had always been blunt and to the point; he had made no secret of his desire for Jacqui Brookes the first night they met. But other than those two dinner invitations she had received from him Brooke Adamson had been shown only his cold disapproval of her.

'It's there again,' he rasped suddenly. 'That fear I saw in your face the other evening.'

'Well, what do you expect me to feel?' Her eyes flashed a warning at him. 'Ever since I first met you you've been insulting and rude. How do you expect me to react to the statement you just made?' she scorned.

'That I want you?' His mouth twisted derisively. 'I expect you to react in an adult fashion. How old are you?' His eyes were narrowed on her pale face.

'Twenty-five.' She deliberately added two years to her age, not wanting to arouse his suspicion in any way.

'And you've been married too, so neither of us are children. What could be more adult than admitting how I feel about you?' He sighed. 'You're right, I have been rude to you in the past—I felt antagonistic towards you from the moment we met almost a year ago. But there was a reason for that.'

'You didn't like me,' she bit out.

He gave her an impatient look. 'On the contrary, I liked you too much. You're the first woman I've wanted in a very long time.'

'But Jocelyn said——'

'That I've had a lot of women in my life,' he finished grimly. "That was true before my marriage, but since

74

then—Perhaps my aunt has believed it to be true since then, it isn't a side of my life I ever discussed with her—with anyone,' he added pointedly. 'There's never been any reason to before. But since I've been away this time I've realised I can't go on like this. Frustration over wanting you is affecting all aspects of my life, including my work.'

Brooke moistened dry lips, hysterically wondering if she was the first woman ever to be propositioned by her own husband in this way. 'I see.'

'I doubt it,' he rasped. 'I apologise for being rude to you in the past,' he added stiffly. "I lose my temper with you in a way I haven't since—since—Jacqui had a way of infuriating me in this way too!'

'I'm sorry.'

'For what?' he snapped.

She shrugged. 'For reminding you of the wife you despised.'

If she thought she had ever seen him angry before she knew now that she never had. His eyes were suddenly like two chips of ice, his nostrils flaring out as his mouth thinned, his face suddenly pale. 'What did you say?' he grated, his lips barely moving as he formed the words.

Brooke backed away in the face of such cold fury. What had she said, for goodness' sake? What could she have said that would induce him to such feelings? It was public knowledge—very public!—that Rafe had hated and despised his wife.

'How dare you presume to know how I felt about Jacqui?' he ground out at her dazed silence, his eyes blazing with fury now, his hands clenched into fists at his sides. 'Don't ever mention my wife again,' he warned savagely.

'But——'

'I may have admitted I want you, Brooke,' he snapped in decisive tones. 'May want to share your bed more badly than anyone since——' he broke off, breathing hard in his anger. 'But I will not have you talking about my wife in the way you just did, and certainly not *guessing* how I felt about her!'

To say she was surprised by his vehemence would be an understatement—she was stunned. How *dared* he act this way? He had thrown her out of his life as if she were a toy that no longer amused him, had publicly humiliated her until he left her with nothing, not even her pride. She didn't have to *guess* how he felt about her, she had lived and breathed his hate for the last three years, indeed it had been that hate and the wish to see her son again that had brought her through the car accident that should have killed her. She *knew* how he felt about her!

'You told the world how you felt, Rafe,' she scorned coldly, 'the day you took her son away from her. Only a cruel and vicious man could have done that to a mother,' she added bitterly.

His head went back in challenge. 'Is that what you think I am, cruel and vicious?' he asked softly—too softly.

But Brooke was past caring about the danger threatening in his voice; she was enraged by the way he had told her he desired her and then turned on her so savagely when she dared to question the feelings he had had for his wife. 'I know it,' she told him defiantly. 'You have no tenderness.' An unbidden picture of Rafe in the nursery earlier with Robert came to mind—and was instantly dismissed. Rafe cared for no one, not even his son. 'No love, for anyone or anything,' she continued determinedly. 'You say you want me, that doesn't involve any feelings other than the baser ones— and I'm not interested, Mr Charlwood. Not in you or your cheap little affair!' Angry blue eyes clashed and held with steely grey ones.

'Perhaps I could persuade you to change your mind?' His voice was still soft.

And still Brooke didn't heed it. 'Never,' she vowed firmly.

His mouth twisted as he walked towards her with slow stealthy steps. 'At least the fear has gone now,' he taunted.

Her chin went high in challenge. 'The more I get to know you, Mr Charlwood, the less I find there is to fear,' she snapped scornfully, determined not to move even when he stood directly in front of her, the heat of his body almost touching hers, the subtle smell of the cologne he always wore mingling with the softness of her perfume.

'Really?' he drawled, taking that last step that moulded his body against hers.

She forced herself not to flinch at the contact. 'Don't try and intimidate me, Mr Charlwood!' she bit out.

'Is that what I'm trying to do?' His strong hands ran lightly up the bareness of her arms, his gaze becoming heated as it roamed over the flushed beauty of her face.

'You know you are!' It took every effort of will to remain calm as his hands still lightly caressed her, his body pressing more intimately against hers.

'Then I'm succeeding, aren't I?' he derided as his hands closed over the rapid pulse in her wrists. 'The scenes I had with Jacqui like this always had one ending,' he murmured throatily, his hands on her waist now, drawing her closer.

Hot colour flooded her cheeks as she too remembered the fierce lovemaking that had always concluded their arguments in the past. 'I thought you said we weren't to talk about your wife,' she reminded him shakily, disturbed by the thoughts he had evoked.

'Aren't you interested in how they ended?' His warm breath fanned her temples.

She swallowed hard. 'I can guess!'

'But it would be so much more enjoyable to show you.' His arms tightened painfully about her. 'You seem to enjoy putting yourself in my wife's place concerning my son, let's see if you can tell me why she preferred the attentions of Greg Davieson to *this*!' Before she could utter a word of protest his mouth had ground down forcefully on hers.

Her first panicked thoughts as he kissed her were, would he know who she really was, would he guess the truth? Surely after living—and sleeping—with a woman for a year and a half he would know he was kissing that same woman!

She held herself rigidly in his arms as his mouth moved sensuously over hers, offering no response but not fighting him either, waiting for the world to come crashing down on her shoulders as he discovered she was his wife Jacqui.

He was breathing hard as he lifted his head, his eyes dark with puzzlement. 'It can't be . . .' he groaned dazedly, shaking his head. 'Not again!' He pushed her away from him as if the touch of her burnt him. 'I'm not going to let this happen to me again,' he told her fiercely.

'Rafe——'

'No, don't touch me!' He backed away from her, the flush of desire fading to leave him pale and haggard. 'Only your eyes are the same,' he said raggedly. 'So how can it be?'

The world seemed to sway on its axis as she waited for his wrath to engulf her.

'I thought it was you I wanted,' he seemed to be speaking to himself. 'But it's because you're like her.' He stared at her in horror. 'God, if I closed my eyes you could be her!'

He hadn't realised the truth! It was hard to contain her excitement. 'Her?' she prompted, already knowing the answer—although Brooke Adamson couldn't be expected to!

'Jacqui!' he groaned. 'You feel like her, *taste* like her!'

She swallowed hard, biting her top lip painfully. 'Does this mean you no longer *want* me?' she scorned.

'You don't understand,' he dismissed flatly. 'No one ever understood, not even her.'

'I'm sure she understood you perfectly, Mr Charlwood,' she told him with controlled contempt. 'And to answer your question,' she met his gaze steadily as he looked at her with tortured eyes, 'I've never met Mr Davieson—but I'm sure *any* man could show more sensitivity than you just gave me!'

His harshly indrawn breath was his only reply before he turned sharply and left—leaving a badly shaken Brooke behind him!

She sat down before her legs no longer supported her. Rafe's suspicions about her identity hadn't been roused, he just despised himself for finding her attractive when she reminded him of the wife he had hated. She doubted that in future she would have any more such advances being made by him—the last thing he wanted was to become involved in any way with a woman who could remind him of Jacqui!

She had been right to assume she wouldn't see any more of Rafe for a while—but again she didn't see Robert either. It was ridiculous, but if she didn't see the father then she couldn't see the son either! She had no idea what she could do about the situation, probably still wouldn't have known if Rosemary hadn't called to see her.

After her last bitchy encounter with the other woman she was more wary than ever as she invited her in.

'What on earth do you do with yourself here all day?' Rosemary looked at her disdainfully, as elegant as ever in a pale lilac dress that fitted smoothly over the perfection of her figure.

Actually Brooke had been wondering the same thing herself, finding that time was dragging heavily on her hands. In London she had gone out to the shops if she became bored, and there had always been Jocelyn to visit or who would visit her. The nearest big town to shop here was almost twenty miles away, and with Jocelyn now gone she spent all of her time alone. Rosemary was the first person she had seen to speak to in the last four days since her emotional scene with Rafe.

She shrugged now. 'I read, watch television, sit outside in the garden. It's very restful here.'

'And boring,' Rosemary concluded dryly, not sitting down as Brooke had invited her to do, her movements as restless as ever.

'I wouldn't go so far as to say that——'

'I would,' the other woman dismissed impatiently. 'Look, did you really mean what you said the other evening, about liking children?' she explained at Brooke's puzzled look.

'Yes . . .'

'Enough to take care of my nephew Robert for this afternoon?'

Brooke's mouth fell open in astonishment. She was actually being *asked* to take care of her son? This was something she had never thought would happen.

'I realise it's an imposition,' Rosemary continued waspishly at her silence. 'But it's the nurserymaid's day off—she's gone off to town or something, and Nanny Perkins has gone down with one of her migraines. I just have to go up to London this afternoon,' she avoided Brooke's curious gaze. 'I have to go and see someone, it's very important,' she added almost defensively.

From her attitude Brooke also had the feeling that the person she was going to see wasn't someone she wanted to discuss. It sounded suspiciously as if Rosemary had an assignation with another man. Not that it was any of her business, and she would be able to spend this unexpected—but welcome!—time with Robert.

'I wouldn't ask you if I weren't desperate.' Rosemary looked at her pleadingly, seemingly unaware of how insulting she had just been.

Not that Brooke minded, all that concerned her was what Rafe would say when he knew she had taken care of his son. Despite her constant requests to him when they met he had never actually given her permission to go near his son again. 'Your brother-in-law——'

'I'll be back long before Rafe gets back from work,' Rosemary dismissed that objection with ease, sensing that victory was in her grasp. 'And Robert has been asking if he might come and see you,' she added enticingly.

Brooke gave her a wide-eyed look. 'He has?' she breathed huskily.

'Yes,' the other woman confirmed with eagerness, aware that Brooke had weakened drastically at the statement. 'Rafe told him to wait until he was asked.'

Knowing full well, after their last parting, that she would be reluctant even to speak to him again, let alone ask permission for his son to visit her!

'If he should happen to get home before I do—a very unlikely occurrence,' Rosemary derided the long hours Rafe worked. 'Just tell him you asked my permission for Robert to come over and I gave it. Oh, you will have him, won't you?' she groaned her desperation. 'If only for a couple of hours.'

She wouldn't have minded if it could have been for a couple of decades, mentally thanking the fates for Connie's day off and Nanny's migraine. 'I'd love to,' she smiled. 'What time shall I call for him?'

'How about now?' Rosemary requested hopefully.

'Now' hardly constituted the afternoon, it was only eleven o'clock! Not that she minded that either, as she nodded agreement. 'I'll walk back with you.'

'Oh, thank you!' The other woman suddenly seemed to realise her uncharacteristic enthusiasm, and her face took on its usual expression of boredom. 'Perhaps I can do you a favour some time,' she added grudgingly.

Brooke knew how desperate Rosemary must have felt about going up to London if she had come to her in this way, having made no effort in the past weeks to hide her dislike. If, as she suspected, Rosemary was going to see another man, that could account for her brittle behaviour the night of the party, it could also account for Patrick's unhappiness. She didn't want to help increase the friction between the other couple by making it possible for Rosemary to meet her lover, and yet the temptation for her to be with Robert was too much for her to refuse. Rosemary and Patrick's marriage was their own affair, she wanted no involvement with any member of the Charlwood family but Robert.

He was out in the garden when they reached the main house, a small area of the smooth green lawn put aside for a sand-box, climbing-frame and slide. One of the gardeners was keeping a protective eye on the little boy as he ran from activity to activity with his usual exuberance, a small bundle of energy in a red and white tee-shirt and navy denims, similar attire to Brooke, the only difference being that her tee-shirt was pale blue.

Rosemary dismissed the gardener and called Robert over to them. With some reluctance the little boy left the sandcastle he had been building to come over to them, his expression lightening as he saw Brooke with his aunt.

'Have you come to invite me to tea?' he asked excitedly, his blue eyes glowing.

His lack of guile was so endearing that Brooke smiled her response. 'I thought we could have lunch first. Then if your aunt isn't back from her visit we can have tea together too.' She glanced at Rosemary for confirmation of her words.

'You would like that, wouldn't you, Robert?' the other woman encouraged.

'Yes,' he replied unhesitant.

'That's loyalty for you,' Rosemary drawled. 'Well, run along with Brooke, Robert, and behave yourself,' she added warningly. 'Otherwise she might not invite you back again. I'll come and collect him as soon as I get back,' she spoke to Brooke now. 'But if I should happen to be a little late perhaps you could bring him back for his bath? One of the maids will put him to bed.'

'Of course,' Brooke agreed in a preoccupied voice, too enthralled by the fact that Robert's hand had crept into the warmth of hers to care that she was being spoken to almost like a servant herself. 'Would you like to go fishing after lunch, Robert?' she asked as they slowly walked back to the cottage together.

He frowned up at her with the intense concentration of the very young. 'I don't have a rod,' he told her gravely.

'We can make some,' she assured him. 'It's quite easy, I used to do it all the time when I was a little bit older than you.'

'Really?' His eyes were wide.

'Yes, really.' She smiled down at him, the sun suddenly seeming brighter, the sky bluer as he returned the smile. 'Now what would you like for lunch?'

'Ice-cream,' came his quick response. 'And chocolate biscuits.'

Brooke laughed softly. 'Maybe for dessert. How about a hamburger to start with?'

'With baked beans?' he asked hopefully.

'My favourite!' she agreed indulgently.

She could almost believe they had always been mother and son as they laughingly prepared the lunch together, Robert laying the table for her, his appetite fierce as he devoured the hamburger and baked beans she had cooked for them with chips, watching with satisfaction as he cleared his plate, requesting the promised ice-cream afterwards, although she remembered how ill he had been the last time he ate here she told him the chocolate biscuits would have to wait until later. He accepted this decision without argument.

He even enjoyed helping her with the washing-up—living in a houseful of servants as he did it was probably a novelty to him!—splashing water over both of them as he stood on a stool next to the sink.

'We're going to be as wet as the fish,' she teased gently as she dried them both off with a towel, and was rewarded for her humour by Robert's enchanting giggle.

He was a delightful child altogether, she learnt as they sat and made the make-shift fishing rods, using a couple of long sticks, some string, a safety-pin bent out of shape for a hook, and bread for bait.

'Do fish like bread?' Robert wanted to know as they walked the short distance to the river.

'Do you?'

'Yes.' He looked puzzled.

'Then why shouldn't the fish?' she teased.

He seemed to accept her grown-up logic, sitting on the river bank next to her as she put the doughy bread on his hook. Not that she actually expected them to catch anything, not even knowing if there were fish in this river. But it was fun, and more than anything else she wanted Robert to enjoy being with her.

She had expected, being only three years old, that he would tire quickly of the fishing, but it seemed he had his father's determination and he was sure he was going to catch a fish. To her surprise he did exactly that!

It was the smallest fish Brooke had ever seen outside of a goldfish-bowl, only about two inches in length, and if a fish could look surprised then this one did! But Robert was ecstatic with his catch, pulling the fish up on to the bank, looking up at her to take it off the improvised hook. The thought of touching the slippery fish filled her with horror, but the thought of letting it struggle until it died horrified her even more.

It was as slippery to the touch as she had imagined it would be, but Robert looked up at her with such hero-worship as she let the fish slide back into the water that it was all worth it.

She looked pointedly at her wrist-watch as Robert seemed intent on re-casting his line. 'I think we should go and get cleaned up now, don't you? Aren't you ready for your tea?' she added at his disappointed expression.

His avaricious appetite warred with the enjoyment he had found in this new activity, and finally the thought of the earlier promised chocolate biscuits won. 'We can come back another day?' he frowned as they packed up their things ready to go back to the cottage.

'If your father says so,' she agreed cautiously, not too sure what Rafe's feelings were going to be, not even sure if he would approve of Robert being with her now.

Robert nodded acceptance of her words, obviously used to this condition being made over his movements. And why shouldn't he be, it was natural for all children to need their parents' permission and approval before they did things. She was just sensitive in this case because it was her son and Rafe was the parent involved, a man she had witnessed being unnecessarily strict with the little boy. But hadn't she also witnessed Robert's joy in having his father home, Rafe's tenderness and love with him in return? Somehow she found it easier to accept that Rafe was too harsh with the little boy; she didn't want to admit that Rafe could have a softer more approachable side than the one she had always known—and hated.

By six o'clock no one had come to collect Robert, so she walked him back to the house herself. She was let in by Shepherd, quickly explaining what had happened

and that she was going to bath Robert and put him to
bed. The butler seemed to find this all slightly unusual,
although he made no demur.

Brooke wouldn't have cared if he had, as she went up
the stairs with Robert, not intending to let anyone spoil
this time of sharing bathtime with her son. To her relief
Robert had no inhibitions about letting her bath him,
having a whole flotilla of boats floating about on the
bubble-topped water. The darkness of his curls clung to
his head damply once she had washed his hair, his little
body was sturdy and strong.

The huge fluffy towel swamped him as she lifted him
out of the bath, and he looked so adorable, so very
young, that she couldn't resist hugging him to her, if
only for a brief moment, while tears clogged her throat.

But she was soon smiling again as Robert produced
the aeroplane-patterned pyjamas he was to wear. She
should have guessed!

'Do you like flying?' she asked as she dressed him
and put him to bed.

His eyes began to glow. 'Daddy sometimes takes me
up in his very own plane.'

Brooke knew about the small jet that Rafe piloted
around England and to the continent; it didn't surprise
her at all that he had been persuaded to take Robert up,
not with the little boy's intense interest in planes. In
fact, that might have contributed to it!

'And I suppose you travel with your daddy
sometimes too?' she queried casually as she arranged
the quilt around him, smoothing back his still damp
curls.

He frowned. 'Not really,' he shook his head. 'I stay
here usually.'

That was what she had thought, what Jocelyn had
always told her. Rafe had been away several times in
the last two months—no wonder Robert was so excited
when he came home!

'Do you have a story-book?' she changed the subject, biting her tongue on any criticism of Rafe, aware that Robert adored his father.

'Noddy,' he said enthusiastically, pointing to the extensive array of books on the small white bookcase along one wall of the room. 'The one about his car, please.'

The book was easily found, and as she began to read it became obvious that Robert knew the story off by heart.

'Daddy often reads to me if I can't sleep,' he explained, looking very young in the child's bed that was still much too big for him.

Again she was being forced to accept that Rafe didn't ignore his son as much as she had thought he did—and she didn't like having to admit that she could have been wrong about him. She knew the hardness in him too well to be deceived.

She could see Robert was beginning to wind down as she continued to read the story, his full day obviously catching up with him as he began to blink tiredly.

'What the——! What are you doing here?'

She looked up at the sound of that rasping voice, flushing guiltily as she saw Rafe had quietly let himself into the nursery, his face a livid mask of fury as he saw her there. She stood up slowly, very conscious of her dishevelment as his sharp gaze moved over her disparagingly. Her hair had been secured in a loose ribbon at her nape before she and Robert went fishing, but the gentle breeze and the exertion of bathing the little boy had released several tendrils about her face, a face completely bare of make-up. But the critical gaze didn't stop there, but moved down to the clinging tee-shirt she wore, a dull red colour entering her cheeks as she followed that suddenly intense gaze, the material clinging damply to her pert breasts where she had got wet bathing Robert. Heavens, she looked almost naked—and she felt it too under that totally male assessment.

'Daddy,' Robert cried excitedly, 'Brooke and I went fishing, I even caught a fish,' he added proudly, sitting up in the bed, all thought of sleep banished at the sight of his father.

The hardness left the steely grey eyes as Rafe looked down indulgently at his son. 'Did you?' His voice had softened too as he walked over to the side of the bed.

'Yes,' Robert glowed. 'Brooke made me a fishing-rod, and I caught a really big fish——'

'Robert!' she reproved lightly, keeping her gaze averted from the daunting figure Rafe made in the navy blue three-piece suit and lighter blue shirt, the waistcoat of the suit fitting flat to his taut stomach.

'Well, perhaps it was only a little fish,' he amended in a deflated voice. 'But I did catch it, didn't I, Brooke?' He looked up at her with beseeching eyes. 'All on my own!'

'You certainly did.' She ruffled his dark curls affectionately.

'And just when did this fishing expedition take place?' Rafe asked his son softly, only Brooke being aware of the underlying steel to his voice.

'This afternoon,' Robert clutched his arms gleefully about his knees. 'I went to Brooke's, and we had hamburgers. And then for tea I had——'

'You spent all afternoon with Brooke?' his father queried quietly.

'Yes,' Robert glowed, still not sensing the tension that surrounded him. 'She makes lovely food, Daddy,' he smiled at the delicacies he had devoured for his tea. 'Can I go over and see her again another day?' he asked hopefully.

'Just for the food?' his father teased.

'Oh no,' Robert answered seriously, not realising he was being gently mocked. 'Brooke's fun, Daddy.'

Cool grey eyes looked over at her. 'Is she indeed?' Rafe drawled.

'Oh yes,' again Robert answered with innocence. 'We got very messy when we were fishing, but Brooke didn't mind a bit. She even touched the wiggly fish,' he grimaced at the thought.

'It would seem you've found yourself a friend.'

As Robert made no attempt to answer the remark Brooke looked up sharply, realising as her gaze clashed with Rafe's that he had been talking to her. Her shoulders straightened at the challenge in his eyes. 'I hope so,' she said defensively.

'I'm sure so,' he drawled. 'Perhaps you wouldn't mind coming outside for a moment? I'd like to talk to you.'

It might have been put as a request, but they both knew it was an order. 'Certainly,' she agreed. 'I'll see you again soon, Robert,' she smiled down at him gently.

'Aren't you coming back to hear my prayers?' He looked up at her beguilingly. 'Nanny Perkins usually does.'

She looked uncertainly at Rafe, not sure how she should answer, not sure if she would be allowed back.

His mouth firmed. 'Brooke will come back in a few minutes. I just want to have a few words with her, okay?'

'Okay,' Robert nodded happily, settling down in the bed again.

Brooke preceded Rafe from the room with some trepidation. He obviously hadn't been aware that she was even in the house, let alone that his son had spent most of the day with her. He didn't seem at all pleased by the fact!

'Where is Nanny Perkins?' he asked curtly as soon as they were outside the bedroom.

She met his gaze steadily, refusing to be cowed by the

anger she sensed in him. 'She had a migraine. And it's the nurserymaid's day off,' she told him before he asked that too.

His eyes narrowed even more. 'Rosemary?'

Now she couldn't quite meet his gaze; her suspicions about his sister-in-law were too revealing. 'She had to go to London,' she dismissed tersely.

'And just where do you come into all this?' Rafe bit out harshly, obviously not satisfied with her abrupt answers.

Her shoulders stiffened at his almost insulting tone. 'I'm the person she asked to take care of your son while she went out,' she informed him tautly.

'Rosemary did?'

She blushed at the disbelief in his tone. 'Well, I didn't kidnap Robert, if that's what you're thinking!' she snapped. 'I'll go and say goodnight to Robert now and then I'll leave,' she added abruptly. 'I'm sure your sister-in-law will confirm what I've told you when she gets back.'

'When,' he nodded grimly, his expression boding ill for the other woman. 'Join me in the lounge for a drink when you've said your goodbyes to Robert.'

She bristled indignantly at his autocratic tone. 'I——'

'Let me re-phrase that,' he said dryly as he correctly read her mutinous expression. '*Will* you join me downstairs for a drink once you're finished up here?' He raised mocking brows.

Her mouth tightened. 'I don't think I'm dressed for that,' she refused with sarcasm—then wished she hadn't as that all-seeing gaze swept over her with complete thoroughness for a second time in a matter of minutes.

'You look just fine to me,' he drawled. 'And I'm sure you agree we've far from finished this conversation?'

She gave an impatient sigh, nodding reluctantly; it hadn't occurred to her that she would have yet another confrontation with him so soon after the last one. 'I'll be down in a few minutes,' she told him stiffly.

'Thank you.' His tone was derisive for her grudging agreement. 'You remember your way back to the lounge?'

'Yes,' she acknowledged dully, watching him stride back downstairs before bracing her shoulders to go and see Robert. Spending time alone with Rafe was the last thing she wanted—ever.

CHAPTER FIVE

SHE was no less shaken when she came downstairs ten minutes later, her composure shattered completely at Robert's 'and God bless Mummy' at the end of his prayers. No matter what she might have thought, what Jocelyn may have believed, Robert was not being brought up to hate his mother.

'Drink?'

Raf's terse question broke into her thoughts, and she realised she had reached the lounge without even being aware of doing so. Rafe was dressed exactly the same as he had been earlier, and for that she felt grateful; she felt untidy enough already without the added elegance of Rafe in an evening suit.

'I'll have a dry sherry—thank you,' she requested as he seemed to be becoming impatient at her lack of reply.

He moved to pour it for her. Brooke took care not to touch the lean strength of his hand as he held the glass out to her. Something, by the mocking twist of his mouth, he was quick to notice.

He made no effort to move away from her, standing dangerously close. 'I believe I owe you an apology,' he murmured huskily.

Hot colour flooded her cheeks, her hand shaking slightly as she held on tightly to her glass. 'There's no need, I've already forgotten the incident.'

'Incident?' His eyes narrowed to steely slits. 'What incident?'

She raised startled eyes to his. 'Why, the other evening when you—when you——'

'Propositioned you,' he finished dryly. 'But that

92

wasn't what I was apologisng for, Brooke,' he drawled derisively. 'While you were upstairs with Robert just now I received a telephone call from Rosemary to tell me that she and Patrick have both been delayed in London overnight. She confirmed what you told me about Robert.'

Brooke swallowed hard at the error she had made, unwittingly introducing the subject she had hoped most to avoid, that of his desire for her. 'I'm relieved about that,' she hastily swallowed her sherry. 'I have to be going now.'

His hand on her arm stopped her. 'Stay and have dinner with me,' he invited softly, his gaze dark on her face. 'It's the least I can do after you've taken care of Robert for most of the day.'

'I——'

'You haven't changed your mind about being afraid of me, have you?' he challenged.

'No,' she bit out forcefully, moving away from him. 'I'm just not dressed for dinner.'

'We'll be alone, Brooke, and I don't give a damn what you wear.'

Her breath caught in her throat at the savage intensity of his voice. She would be a fool to stay here, and yet to leave would seem as if she were running away. 'Perhaps if I could just tidy myself up . . .?'

'Of course,' he agreed instantly. 'I'll take you upstairs to one of the bathrooms and you can freshen up while I go in and say goodnight to Robert.'

The bathroom was well equipped for her needs. She loosened her hair to brush it silkily about her shoulders. The healthy glow of her face needed no adornment, while her tee-shirt and denims were very casual but at least they were dry now.

Her own casualness wasn't so noticeable when she rejoined Rafe downstairs. His jacket and waistcoat were now discarded, as was his tie, his collar loosened, the sleeves of his shirt turned back to just below his elbows.

Her mouth twisted. 'Trying to make me feel more comfortable?' she mocked.

'On the contrary,' he drawled. 'Trying to make *me* feel more comfortable. Do you have any idea what it's like to have to be impeccably dressed all the time?'

'You don't have to be.'

'Don't I?' he mocked. 'I doubt my employees would respect me if I went to work in denims.'

'You should try it some time,' she taunted, finding him much more approachable dressed like this. And that wasn't something she wanted at all! 'It might make you seem more——' she broke off, biting her bottom lip self-consciously.

'Human?' he finished softly. 'But I'm human, Brooke. Didn't I prove that the other evening when I made a fool of myself?'

'Is that what you did?' she queried lightly.

'I admitted my desire for you, and then insulted you by saying I couldn't make love to you because you reminded me of my wife,' he reminded her grimly.

Brooke was very pale. 'You—you didn't say that . . .'

'Oh, but I did,' he ground out, his hands thrust into his trouser pockets. 'You don't even look like her,' he added moodily. 'Nothing at all except your eyes.' He seemed to shake off a demon that was haunting him. 'Shall we go in to dinner?' he suggested coolly, straightening his shoulders.

She agreed with eagerness, following him through to the intimacy of the smaller dining-room. She just wanted to eat her meal and get back to the sanctuary of her cottage, grateful for the fact that they had the presence of Shepherd to prevent any personal conversation.

'How was Robert?' she asked interestedly.

'Already asleep.' Rafe gave a half-smile. 'It sounded

as if you had a very full day. Did you really go fishing?'

She smiled at his incredulous tone. 'Yes. We improvised with the rods. But I had no idea there were actually any fish in the river at the back of the cottage.'

'Otherwise you might not have suggested it,' Rafe teased.

'How did you guess?'

'I think it was your expression when Robert said you touched the "wiggly fish".' He was openly laughing at her now.

She grimaced. 'It wasn't very pleasant, but Robert enjoyed it so much I doubt I'll be able to get out of taking him again—with your permission, of course,' she added as she realised just how much she was taking for granted. Just because no harm had come to Robert today, because he had seemed to like being with her, there was no reason for her to assume Rafe would let his son visit her again.

'Of course,' he acknowledged, not committing himself one way or the other. 'Drink some of your wine,' he instructed as he noticed her untouched glass of red wine that had been chosen to accompany their beef.

With an instinctive obedience Brooke picked up the glass, intending to drink the wine, and then she stopped herself as she realised how easily she had fallen into the trap of letting him dictate even her smallest action. 'No, thank you,' she replied firmly, continuing to eat her meal. 'I don't particularly like red wine.'

'Then let me get you a white one. Perhaps a——'

'I don't like wine very much at all,' she refused with a tight smile, remembering the occasions she had accompanied Rafe on rare business dinners and been told by him that it was unsophisticated and unsociable to refuse the wine offered her. Then she had drunk it, now she wasn't prepared to.

'You said nothing of this the other evening when I brought wine to the cottage,' he frowned.

'I was being polite—after all, it was a gift,' she derided. 'But I would prefer water tonight,' she requested politely of Shepherd.

She was aware that the silence had become strained once the butler had absented himself to get her water, and she looked up at Rafe with puzzled eyes. He looked haggard, his eyes almost black, his nose thinned, his mouth an agonised line. Surely her refusal of the wine hadn't angered him this much?

As she watched him he visibly fought for control, finally giving a light laugh. 'She didn't like to drink alcohol either,' he explained.

'Your wife?' she enquired coolly, suddenly tense. 'But surely at all of those near-orgies she was supposed to have attended she must have drunk alcohol?'

'Why do you persist in defending her when you didn't even know her?' he asked raggedly. 'You aren't her long-lost sister that I knew nothing about come to seek revenge, are you?' The question was put mockingly, and yet the steel of his gaze told her he was far from amused.

'Revenge?' She arched dark blonde brows. 'Don't tell me you were actually a little in the wrong yourself in your marriage?'

'I was completely wrong to have married a child!' he rasped harshly.

'Then why did you?' she said hardly, relieved that he didn't seem to have taken seriously his own suggestion that she might be a relative of his dead wife.

'Why do you think?' he dismissed impatiently.

She shrugged. 'You wanted a son to continue the Charlwood empire.'

'I *wanted* a wife,' Rafe bit out forcefully. 'I wanted a woman to share my life and my bed,' he rasped. 'Instead I found I'd married a young girl, a child who wanted money and jewels, all the things that go with being the wife of a rich man. Only she forgot to be a wife,' he added with bitterness.

Brooke had gone very pale at his accusations, knowing it wasn't the truth. She had loved this man with all her heart, had been willing to do anything to make him happy, including losing her own personality to his stronger one. He was the one who had treated her like just another of his possessions, a pretty toy to be pampered and spoilt—as long as it suited him. It had suited him for only a month, then the need for a son and heir had become most important to him, with her as the vessel to give him that child.

Maybe if she had been the stranger he thought she was she would believe him now, might even have felt sympathy for him. Not that she thought for a moment that that was what he wanted; Rafe had never needed anyone's pity in his life, had never needed anyone for anything!

'Maybe you forgot to be a husband,' she told him tautly.

'What?'

She ignored the icy edge to his voice, meeting the savagery of his gaze with a coolness she was far from feeling. 'You were in your mid-thirties when you met— Jacqui?'

'Yes,' he nodded grim acknowledgement of the fact.

'And you'd never been married before——'

'How do you know that?' he rasped.

Her mouth twisted. 'If you had that would have been in the newspapers too,' she derided.

His eyes were narrowed to steely slits. 'What is the point you're trying to make?'

'I——' she broke off self-consciously as Shepherd returned with the iced water, thanking him with a smile as he poured it for her. 'I don't believe now is the time to discuss this,' she said awkwardly to Rafe.

He nodded acceptance of this fact, although neither of them ate much more, both seeming lost in their own thoughts. Brooke just wanted to get away from here, wished she had never started this conversation; Rafe was sure to want to continue it—and she really had no idea what 'point' she had been trying to make. It just seemed to her that Rafe had never looked at their marriage from her point of view, had only been concerned that she didn't embarrass him with her youth in front of his family and friends, that she made herself as inconspicuous as possible when he didn't need her to act as his hostess.

'I take it your alcoholic dislikes do not also include brandy?' He stood pointedly next to the tray of drinks and glasses once they had returned to the lounge.

She had never been particularly keen on the drink, but after the ordeal she had just been through—sharing an intimate dinner with her husband after two and a half years!—she needed something to steady her nerves. 'I love it,' she lied brightly.

Rafe gave her a rather sceptical look for her unwarranted enthusiasm before turning back to pour two large measures of the dark alcohol into the bulbous glasses, bringing them over to sit at her side on one of the sofas, watching as she took her first sip of the fiery liquid.

She forced herself to show no reaction as the brandy passed smoothly down her throat, holding back a gasp as the vintage alcohol hit the pit of her stomach, feeling the warmth spread through her whole body.

Rafe relaxed back against the cushions, the heavy brocade curtains pulled at the windows in the same material as the sofa they sat on, another large sofa and two chairs placed about the room. It was a beautiful room, but it could certainly never be called cosy. 'You were saying at dinner?' he prompted softly.

'Sorry?' She pleaded ignorance, needing time to get her thoughts together, the brandy making her brain seem fuzzy.

His mouth twisted sardonically. 'We were discussing the reason for the breakdown of my marriage,' he reminded dryly.

Her attention was suddenly centred on the dark liquid swirling in the bottom of her glass, taking a delaying sip. 'I believe it was *reasons*, in the plural,' she finally answered him, her head back as she met his compelling gaze.

He gave an arrogant inclination of his head. 'I believe you were just pointing out that it might have been *my* age that was at fault.'

She flushed at the mockery in his tone. 'You don't think it could have been?'

'This is your theory,' he taunted.

'And it was your marriage,' she snapped. 'You don't seem to give a damn!' She stood up to move across the room, turning to glare at him when she reached the unlit fireplace.

'Oh, I give a damn, Brooke,' he rasped, still sitting on the sofa, but as tense as a coiled spring. 'There just isn't anything I can do about it now.'

'You could stop hating your wife!'

He didn't move a muscle at the accusation. 'I stopped hating her long ago,' he stated flatly.

Brooke paled to actually hear him express the emotion about her. All his actions after the evening she had disobeyed him and appeared in the Greg Davieson show had indicated as much, but she had never actually heard him admit it before. It still had the power to shake her after all this time.

'So what was wrong with my age when I got married?' he prompted at her silence. 'I was too old?'

'Don't be ridiculous! And don't patronise me either,' she snapped irritably. 'I was merely trying to point out that your wife's youth might not have been the only problem.'

'I'm aware of that,' he derided.

Her eyes flashed deeply blue as she glared at him. 'At thirty-five you had an established life, and lifestyle, here at Charlwood, and your business. In fact, your life probably ran like a well-oiled cog.'

'You make it sound boring,' he frowned.

'And wasn't it?'

'For Jacqui, obviously yes,' he moved restlessly, his expression bitter. 'My marriage lasted a total of eighteen months, but it had ended long before that.'

'Did it ever start? A marriage is a partnership, giving and taking on both sides. I doubt you gave very much!' she added with remembered bitterness.

'How is it that you think you know so much about my relationship with my wife?' he demanded tersely. 'What was your own marriage like, your husband?'

'I was young, he was a lot older. He was established in a career and lifestyle, I was immature, still looking for my niche in life,' she told him flatly. 'I thought I'd found it when we were married, but there was no room in his life for a wife.'

'And?'

She gave him a startled look. 'And?'

'Yes.' He told her gaze steadily.

She swallowed hard, wanting to break that gaze but unable to. 'And I loved him, beyond life,' she admitted as if the words were forced out of her. As in fact they were! She had had no intention of telling Rafe one thing about her past life—she was too afraid of exposure, of this man's astute and vindictive mind.

'I didn't realise we had so much in common.' The rasp of Rafe's voice brought her back to an abrupt awareness of her surroundings—and him.

She schooled her features into an expression of boredom. 'Two broken marriages don't mean we have a lot in common,' she dismissed. 'They just mean we're both fallible. I have to go now,' she added curtly. 'Thank you for dinner, Mr Charlwood——'

'Rafe,' he corrected mockingly, standing up in fluid movements.

'Are you sure you should allow me that familiarity?' she taunted him. 'The next thing you know I'll be asking for the use of the family jewels!'

'Ask away,' he invited softly.

Brooke put her brandy glass down, ignoring his gruffly spoken flirtation. She had meant to mock him, not encourage his interest, even the thought of the Charlwood diamonds was enough to nauseate her, one partieular item of it especially. Rafe had insisted she wear the family heirlooms whenever they attended formal occasions, having had the magnificent diamonds reset into a modern style for her shortly after their marriage. The party of a friend, Sir Peter Hamille, had been one of those occasions, and Sir Peter had singled her out for his rakish attention from the beginning of the evening. Maybe she had encouraged him a little because of an argument with Rafe before they left the house, but as Rafe continued to glower at her throughout the evening she began to feel more and more apprehensive of the time when they returned home, alone. The tempestuous scene that followed had been everything she had dreaded—Rafe storming into her bedroom as she was undressing, throwing her down on the bed as he branded her as his exclusive property, the Charlwood necklace twisted about her throat as he held her beneath him, hurting her with the savagery of his lovemaking.

She had borne the bruises of his attack for days afterwards, but the marks the diamonds had made on her throat had taken weeks to fade. Just the thought of that necklace now made her feel panicked, threatened.

Her hand moved to her throat in an unconsciously

protective gesture. 'I think I should be going——'

'Why?'

She gave a nervous smile. 'I have a mountain of things to do at the cottage.'

'Name one.' He watched her tensely.

'I—Well, I——' She couldn't for the life of her think of anything! She and Robert might have had fun this afternoon, but Robert had more than helped her clean up the cottage and himself. She couldn't think of anything she had to do when she got home.

'That's what I thought,' Rafe drawled at her lack of an answer. 'You don't like talking to me?'

'I——'

'Because I like talking to you,' he continued as if she hadn't attempted to answer. 'Sometimes it's easier to—understand the past, when you talk about it.'

'You mean you didn't understand it before?' she scorned.

'Not completely, no,' he replied coldly. 'Did you?'

Brooke gave him a startled look. 'Did I what?'

'Always realise and understand the mistakes you made in your marriage,' he derided.

Brooke became flushed. 'If I had I wouldn't have made them. Sometimes you do something, make a mistake without realising how deeply it affects someone else.'

'Yes,' he agreed heavily. 'I——'

'Here again, Miss Adamson?' mocked a shrill voice. 'You seem to be making a habit of it,' Rosemary taunted.

Brooke turned slowly to look at the other woman, the high flush to Rosemary's cheeks, the dangerous glitter to her eyes telling of the reckless mood that she had sensed from the shrill tone of her voice. Rosemary Charlwood wasn't in a pleasant frame of mind, the charming mood of this morning completely erased.

'Rosemary,' Rafe frowned at his sister-in-law. 'I thought you were staying in town tonight?'

The green eyes took on a feverish gleam as Rosemary glared at him. 'So did I,' she rasped. 'But Patrick had other ideas.'

Rafe glanced behind her. 'He's with you?'

'No,' her mouth twisted. 'He's decided that London suits him better.'

Rafe gave Brooke a look of puzzled exasperation, giving the impression that he was far from pleased at having to deal with the mercurial temperament of his sister-in-law.

Brooke met his frown with one of her own, forgetting her own desperate need to leave seconds ago as she recognised the deep emotional stress of Rosemary Charlwood. She had a right to recognise it; hadn't she been in a state of emotional turmoil herself since her first meeting with Rafe four years ago! Brooke knew enough of that state of mind to realise Rosemary was near to breaking point at this moment, that just a wrong word or gesture could set her off—and Brooke's own presence here was far from helping the situation. Rosemary's anger was all directed at her. But there was no way she could make her excuses and leave at this moment without drawing even more attention to herself.

'Suits him better?' Rafe repeated slowly, his eyes narrowed to icy grey slits. 'The two of you have argued?'

Rosemary gave a disgusted snort. 'Nothing so dramatic,' she scorned, throwing her jacket down on the nearest chair, her black clutch-bag quickly following it. 'Could I have a brandy, please?' She looked challengingly at Rafe. 'A large one,' she added as he moved to pour the requested drink, her eyes as hard as the emeralds they resembled.

Rafe faltered only slightly, filling the bulbous glass with a large measure before turning to hand it to his sister-in-law. 'Do you feel like telling me what you and Patrick have—disagreed about?' he prompted softly.

The green eyes glittered with anger as Rosemary
threw back her head to swallow most of the brandy
down, her anger and tension such that she didn't even
flinch. 'I hardly think this is the time, Rafe,' she shot
Brooke a resentful glare. 'Miss Adamson can't possibly
be interested in our family squabbles.' Her mouth twisted
with spite as she turned to look fully at Brooke. 'Your—
baby-sitting wasn't supposed to have extended to the
father, Miss Adamson,' she bit out harshly, a high flush
to her cheeks as the alcohol began to take effect.

'Rosemary——'

'I can see I'm intruding,' she continued in that high-
pitched voice that was tremulously near to cracking,
slamming her empty glass down on the table before
spinning on her heel to almost run from the room and
up the stairs, a door slamming shut seconds later to
further startle the stunned silence between the two
people she had left behind her.

For once Brooke saw Rafe at a loss for words,
staring after his sister-in-law as if her behaviour was
completely incomprehensible to him. And perhaps it
was. When he and Jacqui had argued in the past if they
hadn't ended it by making love then Rafe would simply
go to his study or the office until her mood passed and
she was ready to behave like a wife to him again. Her
anger at him hadn't usually lasted long!

He gave a deep sigh now, putting his brandy glass
down beside Rosemary's. 'I've had enough of my own
domestic disputes without having to deal with my
brother's.' His scowling comment only confirmed
Brooke's impression of his impatience with both
Rosemary and Patrick for putting him in this awkward
position.

Brooke gave him an unsympathetic look. 'Your
sister-in-law needs to talk to someone,' she told him
softly.

'Me?' he sighed again.

She shrugged. 'There doesn't seem to be anyone else.'

'True,' he acknowledged dryly. 'I'd better go up to her.' His gaze was searching on her face. 'I shouldn't be long.'

Brooke didn't answer him. She didn't care how long he was; she didn't intend being here when he returned. She had no idea what had managed to so upset Rosemary that she had returned home in that state— unless Patrick had discovered his wife's meeting with another man!—but her timely interruption had made it possible for Brooke to leave, something that Rafe hadn't been making easy before her arrival.

She stiffened as Rafe moved closer to her, so near now she could feel the warmth emanating from his body, feel his brandy-scented breath on her cheek. She forced herself to look up at him with unblinking blue eyes, refusing to step back as she wanted to do. She almost gave in to that impulse as long tapered fingers moved to gently caress her cheek. She couldn't bear to have him touch her in this way!

'I think you should go to—to Rosemary.' She swallowed hard, wishing him far away from her, her lashes fluttering nervously over wide blue eyes.

'Yes,' But his thoughts seemed to be far from Rosemary and her problems, his gaze fixed on the moistness of her parted lips. 'Brooke . . .!'

She flinched away from the ragged fierceness of his voice. 'Rosemary,' she reminded him tautly.

His face tightened with displeasure, his hand falling back to his side. 'You're right,' he nodded grimly. 'I should go and talk to her. Wait for me?'

Once again Brooke didn't answer him, waiting only as long as it took him to stride out of the room— completely confident she wouldn't make a move now he had instructed her not to!—to turn and leave the Charlwood house, feeling much as she had the last time she had run from Rafe—terrified! And this time she was running away from his desire, not his anger, although she knew from experience that both could be devastating.

As she showered and prepared for bed she determinedly didn't think of her own reaction as Rafe had touched her, or of her shiver of apprehension as his gaze seemed fixed on her mouth.

The knock on the cottage door fifteen minutes after her return wasn't unexpected, just unwanted. The promise of passion in deep grey eyes had been too intense to be ignored tonight; she should have known he wouldn't be put off by her sudden departure during his absence.

Her blue silky nightgown and négligé were hardly suitable attire to go and talk to him in the circumstances, but she had no intention of dressing again just because of Rafe. That would be too much like admitting the fear curling in the pit of her stomach. She did, however, release her hair from the loose ribbon at her nape, feeling less juvenile that way.

Rafe was still in his shirt-sleeves as she opened the door just far enough to identify him in the light reflecting outside from behind. her. He raised dark brows at her lack of welcome, his mouth twisting mockingly.

'How is Rosemary?' she asked politely.

'Impossible!' he grimaced, his dark hair ruffled by the light breeze outside, revealing the many strands of silver in its thickness. 'She refuses to tell me what's wrong, and when I telephoned Patrick a few minutes ago he was no more forthcoming.'

'He's at the apartment in London?' Still Brooke kept him standing outside. She remembered the apartment very well; it was where she and Rafe had spent their first two happy weeks together before they were married, had remained the only place they could go where Rafe would be completely relaxed and natural. She had fond memories of that apartment.

'Yes,' Rafe dismissed tersely. 'I didn't expect you to leave the house the way you did.'

'I had no reason to stay,' she shrugged.

'Then would you mind if I came in?'

'It's late——'

'It's ten-thirty at night,' he mocked. 'I've seen the cottage lights on much later than that.'

A dark flush coloured her cheeks. 'You've been spying on me!'

'Not really.' He shook his head, finally taking the initiative to push the door open and enter without her invitation, closing the door softly behind him as she stepped back. His gaze moved warmly over her face and body as she stood bathed in the light of the single lamp that burned in the lounge, a hungry look on the sharp planes of his face as he looked down at her. 'The windows of my study face this way,' he rasped. 'I've often looked over here—and wished I could join you.'

'Rafe——'

'God, but you're beautiful!' He stepped closer to her, pulling her relentlessly against him, his hands gentle and yet firm through the silky material of her négligé.

'Looks aren't everything, Mr Charlwood.' Brooke tried to hold herself back from him, but the warmth of his body through the silky material of his shirt brought the memories flooding back, the lean strength of his chest and arms making her feel weak.

'I know that, Brooke,' he said raggedly, his lips blazing down her arched throat, his tongue outlining the curve of her ear before he bit gently on the lobe. 'I don't want to just look at you,' he groaned, easing the négligé from her shoulders to fall unheeded at their feet as he caressed the skin he had bared with moist lips. 'I want to touch you, I want to *feel* you, want to know you want me as much as I want you. Brooke . . .!' His mouth at last moved to claim hers.

Their surroundings disappeared, the world outside no

longer existing, they were just a man and woman who had been denied each other for too long, desire burning to a flame the moment their mouths moved together, drinking their fill of each other with greedy delight.

Rafe trembled with anticipation as her shaking fingers released the buttons on his shirt as she sought closer contact with him, shuddering his reaction as she caressed the dark hair there, her fingertips encountering the hardened male nipples. 'Dear God . . .!' he groaned, his mouth opening hungrily over hers.

Her knees went weak at the intimacy, and her lips slipped away from his mouth as she rested her cheek against the dampness of his chest. She knew she should stop this, knew it had to be stopped, and yet she couldn't move away from him, at last had to admit to herself the emotion that had been hovering on the edge of her subconscious ever since Rafe had touched her earlier. She still wanted him, physically responded to him, even after all he had done to her in the past. He had publicly humilated her, lied about her morality, denied her Robert, and *still* she could respond to his slightest touch. Now she had reason to fear herself!

'Brooke?' Rafe sensed her bewilderment, his hand beneath her chin as he tilted her face up towards him.

She moistened her suddenly dry lips. 'Rafe, I——'

'Please don't,' he pleaded huskily, moulding the contours of her body to his, making her fully aware of how deeply aroused he was. 'Don't analyse what we have, just accept it. I've waited almost three years to find a woman I could even think of making love to, please don't say no now I've found you!'

Three years? But surely he—Brooke was given no more time for thought, to delve the shock of realising Rafe hadn't wanted another woman since Jacqui, his mouth possessing hers in open hunger, searching beyond the sweetness of her lips once again to ignite her desire.

'You're beautiful, so beautiful,' he murmured throatily as he lowered her softly to the carpeted floor, easing the nightgown from one shoulder as he lay her back on the discarded négligé. His hands framed her face as his lips paid homage to each beautiful feature, moving with butterfly caresses over each eyelid, down the straightness of her nose, across each flushed cheek, and finally back to the parted softness of her mouth.

Her fear of herself, her response to a man she should hate, was forgotten as she returned the kiss, clinging to the strength of his shoulders as he leant across her, gasping her pleasure as one strong hand moved to cup her breast, smoothing aside the silky material to expose the rosy tip, his thumb caressing the silken nub until it flowered beneath his touch, hardening until every featherlight caress became a torment of ecstasy for Brooke, her lips parting beneath his till she ached for fulfilment, the throbbing sensuallity of Rafe's thighs as he lay against her telling her that he too needed that sexual hunger satisfied.

'I want you,' he moaned unnecessarily, his lips moist and arousing as he moved down the length of her body, his mouth closing possessively over her hardened nipple, loving the sensitive tip until she arched up into him, holding his head against her so that he shouldn't leave her bereft of this dizzying pleasure. 'I can't leave any part of you untouched,' he lifted his head to explain softly, and her groan of dismay at his leaving her quickly changed to a deep moan as her other breast renewed its acquaintance with the only man ever to know her this intimately.

Her fingers lightly grasped the dark hair at his nape, feeling the tautness of his neck, turning her mouth into his as he left her breasts to the tender ministrations of his hands. It was exactly as it had been for them in the beginning, before Charlwood and a wedding ring had ruined everything between them, distrust and fear ripping them apart, love becoming a thing of the past.

Love! Dear God, she couldn't let Rafe do this to her! Rafe had never loved her, and there was no love between them now, only wanting and desire. If Rafe once guessed she was the same woman who had disillusioned him against women the last three years, was the wife he believed had betrayed him, then he would wreak a much worse vengeance on her than she cared to think about.

'Jacqui, what is it?' He raised his head as he sensed her mental withdrawal, his eyes darkening to black pools of disbelief as he realised what he had done. 'Dear God!' he rasped savagely, pushing himself up and away from her, shaking his head in bewilderment.

'What's the matter, Rafe?' She scorned to hide her real feelings of fear. 'Did you close your eyes again and imagine I was your wife?'

He had paled to a ghastly grey colour, his eyes tormented black pools. 'Brooke——'

'Would you just leave?' She turned away to hide the fear she felt.

'I don't—I can't——'

'Will you just go!'

'Dear God, am I to be haunted by her for the rest of my life?' he groaned in a tormented voice as he slowly let himself out of the cottage, leaving a devastated Brooke behind him.

Even physically changed as she was, Rafe's subconscious perisisted in recognising her. How long before his conscious knew her too!

CHAPTER SIX

As with the last time Rafe had left her so abruptly he seemed once again to be avoiding her. Not that she minded that, she had no wish to see him either.

Her fear of him now was of a different kind; she now feared the physical response to him that she had no control over. No matter how many times she told herself she would never respond to Rafe like that again she knew it wasn't true. From the moment she had seen Rafe again almost a year ago she had feared the betrayal of her body. Her heart, she was sure, would have none of him, the mental anguish he had put her through was still raw on her emotions, but physically . . .! The further Rafe stayed away from her in future the better she was going to like it!

But if Rafe had decided to avoid her and the memories she seemed to evoke for him, he made no further effort to stop Robert visiting her. The little boy came to see her daily now, the two of them spending a lot of time in the garden together. Robert's adoration of his father became obvious, the little boy very sad when his father had to go away on his frequent business trips. And those trips seemed more frequent than ever, making Brooke wonder if she had anything to do with his need to get away from Charlwood. Patrick, according to his wife, was still in London, even two weeks after the argument that had brought Rosemary back home in such an emotional state.

'Robert has been asking for you all day.' A disgruntled Rosemary accompanied the little boy over to the cottage one afternoon, seeming pale and drawn in her husband's absence. 'I haven't known what to do with him, he's been so truculent,' she scowled.

Brooke looked down concernedly at her son, noticing the too-bright eyes and the flush to his cheeks. 'Darling, are you feeling all right?' She went down on her haunches beside him, her palm against his forehead. It was burning hot. She looked up at Rosemary. 'Have you taken his temperature?'

'Don't fuss over him, Brooke——'

'*Have* you taken his temperature?' She straightened, still maintaining a hold on one of Robert's clammily warm hands.

The other woman flushed uncomfortably. 'Well, of course I haven't. He's all right, he just wants some attention with Rafe away again.'

Brooke gave her an impatient look, leading Robert gently by the hand into the kitchen, lifting him up to sit on one of the work-tops. 'Do you mind if I lift up your tee-shirt a minute, poppet?' she asked softly, more convinced than ever by the mute nod she received in response that Robert was far from well.

'What are you doing?' Rosemary stood behind her frowning deeply. She was still not overly friendly towards Brooke, although the occasions when she brought Robert over she was usually polite, seeming embarrassed by the scene she had caused the night she walked in on Brooke having dinner with Rafe.

'Feel his forehead,' Brooke muttered before going to the small medicine cabinet she kept down here, taking out the thermometer to put it under Robert's arm; his whole body felt hot and clammy to the touch.

'Oh God,' the other woman mumbled, her expression stricken.

'Am I ill?' Robert instantly picked up the tension in the room. 'Am I going to die and go away like Aunt Jossy and Mummy did?' Wide blue eyes looked at them in sheer panic.

Rosemary suddenly seemed to realise how her behaviour was affecting the child, and she laughed softly, the sound reassuring in itself. 'You might get a few days in bed being pampered and spoilt,' she teased, ruffling his hair affectionately. 'But you certainly aren't going to die.' She glanced worriedly at Brooke as the thermometer was removed and read.

Brooke looked at the reading three times before she could believe it. 'A hundred and two,' she told the other woman raggedly, forcing a bright smile to her lips as she picked Robert up and cuddled him. 'How would you like to go to bed right now?' She was already on her way out of the door as she asked the question, walking quickly towards the house, knowing without looking that Rosemary was at her side.

'Can I have ice-cream?' he asked hopefully, wanting his favourite food even though he must be feeling very ill indeed.

'Maybe after the doctor has been,' she compromised, not at all sure what was wrong with him, let alone whether or not he should be allowed to eat. 'We'll see what he says, hmm?'

He looked disappointed, but he nodded his head in agreement, resting down on her shoulder, his arms about her neck by the time they reached the house. He seemed to have fallen asleep, and his face was flushed and feverish.

'He never does that,' Rosemary told her in a worried voice. 'He has so much energy that the only time he ever falls asleep is when he's put to bed at night. Oh God, he must be really ill!' she groaned as she opened the nursery door for Brooke. 'And I just thought he was being naughty.' Tears glistened in the remorse-filled eyes. 'If anything happens to him——'

'It isn't going to,' Brooke assured the other woman roughly, laying Robert down on the bed. 'Call a doctor,' she instructed Connie as she came in to see what was going on.

Resentful brown eyes looked at her in challenge. The

girl was no more willing to obey her now than she had been in the past.

'I'll call the doctor.' Rosemary took over briskly, once again the haughty mistress of Charlwood. 'And, Connie, you go and get a cloth and bowl of cold water. Well, don't just stand there!' she snapped as she too received no response. 'And bring them straight back to Miss Adamson,' she added as the girl moved hurriedly to the door.

The bowl and cloth appeared with miraculous speed, and Brooke bathed Robert with the cool water until the doctor arrived. Rosemary brought the elderly Dr Wilson up herself. The doctor had been with the Charlwood family for years, having been the one to confirm Jacqui's pregnancy four years ago. As with the Charlwood family there was no recognition in his eyes as he glanced at Brooke Adamson.

Both Brooke and Rosemary stood at the bedside as he made his examination, Nanny Perkins dismissing Connie to take over any fetching and carrying herself. Three years had aged the already elderly woman considerably, although she seemed to have lost none of her energy.

The doctor straightened at last. 'Mumps,' he diagnosed.

'Mumps?' both Brooke and Rosemary echoed dazedly.

'On the left side. See?' He gently turned Robert's face to the right, a slight swelling now visible on the left side of his cheek and jaw. 'Nothing to worry about, old chap,' he assured the wide-eyed little boy. 'You'll just feel a little bit poorly for a few days.'

The doctor might make light of the ailment to Robert, but the adults in the room were all aware of the fact that there could be serious complications to the illness. Rosemary visibly paled, and Brooke had trouble making her shaky limbs support her. The two women followed the doctor from the room as Nanny Perkins helped the little boy change into his pyjamas.

'Someone should be with him all the time until his fever breaks and his temperature starts to drop,' the doctor told him gravely. 'You saw the way I bent his head up at the neck to meet his knees?' He waited for them to nod confirmation. 'Well, if he complains of any pain at the back of his neck, or stiffness in the limbs when you test him like that again I want you to call me immediately. The cases of meningitis in these——'

'Meningitis?' Brooke echoed desperately.

Kind blue eyes flickered over her curiously, although the doctor asked no probing questions. 'It's very rare,' he soothed.

'But possible?' she persisted.

'Yes,' he nodded without preamble. 'Now the important thing is to get his temperature down, reduce the fever.'

Brooke listened attentively as he explained exactly what he wanted done. She wasn't about to let anything happen to her son! 'I'll sit with him first,' she told Rosemary once the doctor had left.'

'You? But——'

'I'll sit with him, Rosemary,' she repeated determinedly, challenge in every bone of her body. If anyone should dare to question her right to sit with her son——!

Puzzlement flickered questioningly in hard green eyes, confusion quickly taking its place as Rosemary looked at her almost with recognition. But the feeling quickly faded, and with a dismissive shrug she nodded. 'If that's what you want. I'll admit that Robert has become very fond of you the last few weeks,' she added grudgingly.

Brooke was still slightly shaken by that brief feeling of familiarity she had sensed in the other woman, although she answered evenly enough. 'Perhaps you could contact Rafe . . .?'

The frown was back in Rosemary's eyes. 'I don't know where he is.'

'Don't know——? Surely he leaves word where he is just in case of an emergency such as this one?' Brooke demanded disbelievingly. Even during their marriage she had always known where he was!

'Patrick will know——'

'Then call him!' Her voice rose in her exasperation.

'I can't,' the other woman choked.

'Rafe will be furious if he isn't told,' Brooke warned.

Contrition shone briefly in over-bright green eyes. 'I just can't talk to Patrick,' Rosemary explained raggedly. 'We parted so badly, said such vicious things to each other,' she shook her head. 'I just can't talk to him,' she repeated dully.

Brooke felt sorry for the other woman; she knew that if Patrick had been one tenth as harsh in their argument as Rafe used to be with her then her reluctance was understandable. 'I'll call him,' she assured Rosemary gently. 'As long as you'll call Rafe,' she added with a self-derisive laugh.

Rosemary gave a rueful smile. 'Deal!'

Brooke's conversation with Patrick was necessarily short and to the point, although what he had to tell her in reply filled her with dismay.

'Rafe's in Australia,' he groaned worriedly. 'Look, I'll call him and then I'll come down myself as soon as possible.' He rang off abruptly.

Rosemary was back in the nursery with Robert, and to her credit she didn't even blink when told of her husband's imminent arrival, but stood up to leave. 'Call me when you want me to take over.' She left the room with a quiet dignity Brooke could only admire, knowing how shaken she must be by the fact that Patrick was coming back to the house.

When he arrived an hour later Brooke could see he had fared no better than his wife from their separation. He was lean and harsh, a coldness in his usually laughing blue eyes. He didn't even ask about Rosemary, greeting the limp Robert with enthusiasm before turning to Brooke. 'He's getting the first available plane.' He wisely didn't mention names in front of the sharp young ears; the knowledge that his father was so far away would have deeply upset Robert, and he was already ill enough. 'But even so ...' Patrick added pointedly.

'Yes,' she sighed, knowing that it would be the next evening at least before Rafe arrived back at Charlwood. They were going to reach the critical time in Robert's illness long before that. Well, she was Robert's mother, she would bring him through it. 'Er—Rosemary is in your bedroom,' she gave Patrick a searching look, watching as a shutter came down over his emotions. There might be little physical resemblance between the two brothers, but in that moment he looked very like Rafe. 'Patrick——'

'What has she told you?'

Brooke glanced pointedly down at Robert, nodding to the man at her side to precede her out of the room as she saw the little boy had drifted off to sleep again, a high flush to his cheeks, the swelling of one side of his face becoming more noticeable by the minute. She closed the door softly behind them, looking up at Patrick with compassionate eyes. 'Rosemary hasn't told me anything,' she put a consoling hand on his arm, 'but I know things aren't good between you at the moment.'

'Good!' He gave a harsh derisive laugh. 'That has to be the understatement of the year!'

'Patrick——' she broke off as a door opened further down the corridor, and Rosemary's face became stricken, and then accusing, before she slammed back into her bedroom. 'Oh dear,' Brooke ·groaned her dismay. 'I'm afraid she's misunderstood—Will you go to her?' she asked Patrick with concern.

His jaw was clenched, a pulse beating erratically in his jawline. 'I'm staying only as long as it takes for Rafe to get here, then I'm returning to London.'

'And Rosemary?'

He stiffened. 'Rosemary has a few problems of her own to sort out. I think she can do that better alone.'

'But, Patrick——'

'I'm sorry, Brooke,' he bit out forcefully, his eyes flashing a warning. 'I know you mean well, but what's between Rosemary and myself—well, it's between us.'

'She's upset——'

'So am I,' he grated. 'Look, I need to shower and change,' he ran a weary hand through the sandy fairness of his hair. 'If you need me I'll be in the spare bedroom just opposite here.'

She watched as he moved to the bedroom with decisive movements, several doors away from the room he usually shared with his wife. She shook her head. Whatever was wrong between the other couple she no longer thought it was because Rosemary was having an affair; the other woman had reacted too strongly to seeing Patrick talking to her for her to be guilty of having a lover herself. But they had enough problems between them without Rosemary jumping to the wrong conclusion about what she had just witnessed.

She knocked lightly on the other woman's bedroom door, entering immediately, her expression softening as she saw the way Rosemary hurriedly wiped the evidence of tears from her cheeks, sitting up primly on the side of the bed to compose her features into their usual arrogance.

'Robert is asleep,' Brooke told her lightly. 'I wondered if you would mind sitting with him for a few minutes while I go over to the cottage and get myself a few things for overnight.'

Rosemary seemed to pale even more, her eyes shadowed. 'Overnight . . .?'

Brooke nodded briskly. 'I'm going to stay with Robert tonight.'

Rosemary visibly bristled with indignation. 'I'm grateful for your help, Miss Adamson, but I really think you're taking too much upon yourself. Robert has a nanny, a nurserymaid, and myself, he doesn't need anyone else.'

Brooke's eyes became steely as she steadily held the other woman's gaze. 'I'm staying with Robert, Rosemary.'

Dull colour entered the other woman's cheeks. 'I don't think——'

'I'm staying, Rosemary,' she repeated in a cold voice, her head back in challenge.

That look of dawning familiarity was back in the puzzled green eyes. Rosemary gave her a searching look, and Brooke was once again aware of the feeling of recognition. But she didn't care about that now, Robert was all that mattered to her. 'Are you going in to sit with him?' she demanded impatiently. 'Or shall I ask Nanny Perkins to do it?'

'Of course I'll go in and sit with him, he's *my* nephew,' Rosemary snapped defensively.

Her mouth twisted. 'I'm well aware of that. I shouldn't be long,' she added lightly. 'Rafe's expected back from Australia tomorrow,' her voice unconsciously sharpened. 'Patrick will be staying in one of the spare rooms until then,' she told her gently. 'Rosemary——'

'It's none of your business what the sleeping arrangements are between my husband and myself,' the other woman snapped, standing up with an angry swish of the blue pleated skirt she wore with a contrasting cream blouse.

'I agree,' Brooke said quietly, with sincerity. 'It isn't.'

Uncertainty flickered across the haughty features, the

controlled mask breaking once again. 'Earlier, when I——' she broke off, chewing awkwardly on her inner lip. 'You and Patrick——'

'He's concerned about Robert, we all are.'

'Yes. Yes, of course,' Rosemary answered with relief. 'I just—I'm sorry for what I—thought,' she said abruptly, unable to meet Brooke's gaze.

'He's also disturbed by the situation between the two of you——'

'A situation *he* caused,' Rosemary burst out angrily.

'I don't know anything about the problem between the two of you,' Brooke soothed gently. 'But I want you to know that if you ever do feel in need of someone to talk to I'm here.'

Rosemary gave her a resentful glare. 'As I've said, it's none of your business.' She moved to the door. 'I'll make arrangements for a cot-bed to be put up in Robert's room for you for tonight. As you insist on staying,' she added waspishly.

Brooke didn't even try to push the matter of Patrick and Rosemary's estrangement any further. She had made her position clear, as a possible listener to one or both of them, the rest was up to them.

Patrick received a brief telephone call from Rafe late that evening telling him he had managed to get a flight and would hope to be back at Charlwood late the following evening. Somehow just knowing Rafe was on his way filled Brooke with a confidence that everything was going to be all right now, that Robert would get better quickly.

When his temperature rose to a hundred and three during the night she began to have her doubts, sponging him down with cold water as the doctor had instructed her to, leaving him with no clothes on at all in an effort to bring his temperature down to normal. As witness to how ill he must be, Robert slept through the whole uncomfortable experience, shivering in spite of his raised temperature, looking suddenly very small and vulnerable.

The cot-bed that had been brought in for Brooke and placed against the opposite wall remained unused as the night progressed, continuing to minister to Robert as the hours slowly passed. Then finally about five o'clock she noticed a slight drop in his temperature, an even slighter easing of his disturbed breathing, finding fresh energy herself as she continued to bathe him, almost crying with relief when she found there was none of the terrifying stiffening of the joints the doctor had warned them about.

Patrick and Rosemary checked on her periodically throughout the night, although she refused to relinquish Robert's care to either of them.

By seven o'clock, when a slightly ruffled Nanny Perkins insisted she take over now, Brooke was feeling quietly triumphant. Robert's temperature was down to a hundred, and his face was not quite as flushed.

'I thought you might like to go down and have some breakfast.' The older woman was still resentful at the way she had been superseded by Brooke with her charge, although she had been powerless to object to Brooke's presence when the weakened little boy had woken up during their exchange and asked for Brooke to stay with him. The request had warmed Brooke, but she could understand how hurt the older woman must have felt.

She didn't want any food, but after her sleepless night a cup of coffee sounded inviting. She stood up stiffly, having occupied the small nursery chair when she wasn't actually sitting on the side of Robert's bed. 'That would be nice, thank you,' she accepted softly.

Nanny Perkins snorted her disapproval. 'I'm sure I can manage here.'

Brooke held back her smile, knowing this was no time for levity. This woman had had her feathers ruffled by Robert's preference for what appeared to be a relative stranger. Nanny Perkins couldn't possibly know of the invisible maternal bond that drew the woman and child irresistibly together. 'I'm sure you can,' she nodded seriously. 'Although you will call me if there's any change?' Fear once more leapt into shadowed blue eyes.

The older woman's face softened momentarily as she forgot to be resentful for a few moments. 'Yes, I'll call you,' she said huskily. 'Now run along and get some food inside you,' she instructed waspishly as she realised her lapse.

The food did seem quite appetising once Brooke reached the dining-room and saw the breakfast foods laid out in silver warming salvers. She helped herself to some bacon and mushrooms before seating herself opposite the morose-looking Patrick.

'How's Robert?' he enquired moodily, looking as if he hadn't slept at all either.

'Better, I think.' She poured a cup of coffee for herself, noticing that Patrick seemed to prefer just that, having no food himself. 'The doctor will be along later, we'll know more then.' Some of the buoyancy left her as she considered what the doctor might say when he arrived.

Patrick seemed to shake off his own problems for a moment, giving her a considering look. 'You seem— very fond of him.'

It took tremendous effort to continue eating normally; she had suddenly lost her appetite. 'He's an endearing child,' she answered at last.

'Yes,' he acknowledged thoughtfully. 'But even so——'

'Is Rosemary not joining us?' She was deliberately provocative, knowing she had succeeded in diverting him as his mouth tightened and his eyes frosted over.

'I've been informed by one of the maids that she is

breakfasting in her room,' he replied stiltedly, standing up noisily. 'If you'll excuse me,' he muttered before striding out of the room.

Rosemary spent most of the day upstairs, leaving her room only on the occasions she sat with Robert, the three women, Nanny Perkins, Connie, and Rosemary taking it in turns to sit with the little boy during the morning while Brooke rested in one of the spare bedrooms. But she couldn't sleep, and as soon as she heard the doctor arrive she ran down the corridor to Robert's room to hear his verdict.

'The worst of it appears to be over,' he diagnosed cheerfully. 'Mrs Charlwood tells me you're the one who has been caring for him, Miss Adamson,' he looked at her beneath bushy grey eyebrows. 'You've been an excellent nurse.'

A dark blush stole up her cheeks. 'Thank you,' she mumbled.

He gave her a fiercely probing look. 'Although a little sleep for yourself wouldn't come amiss now, I think,' he told her sternly.

'I've promised Robert I'll read him a story,' she smiled at her son, receiving a weak smile of pleasure in return. 'I can't disappoint the patient, doctor.' She looked up challengingly.

His expression remained stern. 'As long as you don't become a patient yourself.'

Her smile deepened. 'I'll try not to.' In spite of her lack of sleep she didn't feel in the least tired, and spent most of the day with Robert despite protestations from almost everyone that she would tire herself out.

'Will Daddy come soon?' Robert asked her early that evening.

She gave him an understanding smile. 'I'm sure he won't be long now, darling,' she squeezed his hand as it lay limply in hers. 'Australia is a long way, you know.'

'Yes,' he sighed, his blue eyes so like her own trusting

on her face. 'Daddy told me. He showed me it in a book once. I wish I could have gone with him, I wouldn't have got ill then.'

'You would, Robert. The doctor told us you'd had the sickness several days before Aunty Rosemary and I even realised you were ill,' she explained, remembering her own guilt when she had been told this. Robert had seemed fine the last three days—a little quiet, but certainly not ill. None of them had realised he had been suffering from mumps for several days before they noticed it.

'But I'm better now,' he persisted.

'Almost,' she nodded, confident it was true.

'Better enough to have ice-cream?' His eyes brightened expectantly.

'*Well* enough,' she corrected with a light laugh. 'And I don't suppose a little ice-cream would hurt you.' In fact, the return of his appetite was welcome; she had only managed to get a little liquid down him the last thirty-six hours.

He felt sleepy again after only a few mouthfuls of the vanilla ice-cream, and he had in fact fallen into a deep sleep by the time she returned from taking the dirty bowl down to the kitchen.

She sat and watched him for a while as he slept, grateful for the chance to take him through this illness, knowing that if Rafe had been at home he wouldn't have let her care for his son. He would probably ask her to leave when he returned later tonight, but he could never take this away from her! This time with Robert, nursing him, had strengthened her bond with him, and it was a bond that she would never let Rafe destroy for a second time. And she was sure he would want to try.

'Would you like me to sit in with him now?'

She turned at the quietly spoken question, her eyes widening as she saw it was Connie, a youthfully resentful Connie. 'No, thank you,' she refused abruptly.

The younger woman chewed on her inner lip, looking uncomfortable. 'Could I get you a cup of tea, then?' she offered awkwardly.

Brooke frowned at this sudden change in attitude. 'You don't have to do that, Connie.'

The blush that coloured the girl's cheeks looked most unattractive against her red hair. 'I know I don't,' she bit out. 'But would you like one?'

Brooke frowned as she realised this was in the nature of an olive-branch! Somewhere during the last thirty-six hours she had gained the grudging respect of both Nanny Perkins and this young woman. Perhaps they sensed how much she too loved Robert; whatever the reason, she had been tentatively accepted by them. 'A cup of tea sounds lovely, thank you,' she gave a bright smile.

'Good,' Connie smiled her relief. 'I won't be long.'

Brooke had no idea how long Connie was getting the tea. She sat down on the cot-bed for a few minutes to wait for the offered tea and knew no more for several hours.

She awoke with a start when she did wake, a heavy weight of oppression telling her subconscious that it should never have let her sleep in the first place. Her stricken gaze instantly flew across the darkened room to the bed a short distance away, her eyes widening as she saw the man sitting in the nursery chair that was too small for his large frame. Rafe was back!

She lay absolutely still, hoping to escape drawing his attention to the fact that she no longer slept, drinking in her fill of him without his knowledge, not yet prepared to face the verbal cruelty they usually engaged in, and too vulnerable after the recent worry of Robert's illness.

She looked at a Rafe who had rarely been visible during their married life together, a man with ruffled dark hair, a haggard look to his face, his clothes casual, a light cotton shirt and close-fitting denims, unusual attire for him at any time; Rafe was a man who lacked his usual self-control and arrogance.

As if becoming aware of her glance he turned to look at her, his eyes gleaming in the light from the single night-lamp as he slowly stood up to come towards her. Brooke hastily pulled herself up into a sitting position, smoothing her hair selfconsciously, smoothing her tee-shirt down over her denims from where it had ridden up her midriff as she slept.

'You're awake,' he said needlessly.

She put her feet to the ground, moistening dry lips. 'Robert?' She still felt incredibly tired, hardly able to focus on the tiny figure in the bed across from her.

'Very well—thanks to you,' he added gravely. 'His temperature is down to normal, and Rosemary assures me the swelling is down a little too.'

'Thank heavens!' They both spoke in whispers, conscious of the sleeping child. 'I—Have you been back long?' She looked up at him with wide eyes, curious as to how long she had been asleep in his presence.

'Just over three hours.' His expression was intense. 'Rosemary told me how you've cared for Robert; I don't know how to express my thanks.'

There was no doubting the sincerity of his tone, and she blushed uncomfortably. 'I don't want or need thanks——'

'Well, you're getting them.' His voice grated with tension, his hands clenched at his sides. 'I'm very grateful for what you've done for Robert, especially considering the manner in which *we* parted when last we met.'

Brooke froze, as if he had actually struck her. 'We may be antagonists, Mr Charlwood,' she bit out, 'but I would never allow that to influence my affection for Robert.'

'We aren't antagonists,' he groaned, sinking down beside her on the bed, his gaze avidly searching her pale face. 'Oh God, *Brooke*!' he murmured raggedly before his head bent and he claimed her mouth in a searching rather than taking kiss. 'I've thought of you every day for the last three weeks,' his mouth moved erotically against her throat, his tongue probing the hollows. 'And I really mean *you*, Brooke!' His mouth claimed hers once again, crushing her against the hardness of his chest, his heart beating erratically against the palm of her hand.

She felt weakened by lack of sleep, unable to fight the waves of desire that were washing over her like a tide. She wanted Rafe, and if she were honest with herself she had thought of him every day for the last three weeks too. This explosion of the senses between them had only been postponed, and now it could be delayed no more.

She sank backwards on the bed, taking Rafe with her, her fingers entangled in the dark thickness of his hair, accepting the homage he was paying her mouth, their lips moving moistly together.

'Dear God, dear God,' Rafe muttered as her hands moved to slowly caress his body, fast spinning out of control, pushing up her tee-shirt to bare her breasts, his hands moving to the buttons of his own shirt, ripping them open as he sought flesh contact with her. He gave a throaty groan as their torsos seared together, moist flesh against moist flesh, the rough hair of Rafe's chest moving erotically against the hardened tips of her breasts.

Another noise other than their own ragged breathing broke into Brooke's hazy thoughts, and she suddenly became conscious of the fact that they weren't alone. Their son was in the room with them! 'Robert!' she gasped her dismay, pushing Rafe away from her to straighten her clothing, not looking at him as she hurried over to Robert's side, too embarrassed to do so, sure he must be regretting this lapse between them too.

Robert had only turned over in his sleep, and was resting normally now, his mouth slightly open. She continued to look down at him, sensing Rafe's presence beside her, too conscious of the fast rise and fall of her breasts to face him.

'Darling——'

'Please, Rafe,' she shook off his hands on her shoulders as he would have pulled her back against him. 'Not here—I can't,' she added raggedly as he seemed about to protest.

His answer was to turn on his heel and forcefully leave the room, closing the door decisively behind him.

Brooke's breath left her with a tremulous sigh. Tonight's encounter with Rafe had been so much more dangerous than ever before, because tonight he had been making love to Brooke Adamson exclusively, his wife completely forgotten.

She turned sharply as the door opened behind her, sighing her relief as she saw it was Rosemary. The last thing she wanted was to see Rafe again right now. And she didn't like to think why she didn't want that.

'I'm going to sit with Robert tonight,' the other woman told her firmly. 'One of the spare bedrooms has been put aside for you.'

Brooke would have liked to argue with Rosemary, tell her that she would be staying right here, but considering the way she had fallen asleep earlier when she should have been watching over Robert she knew it was best if she got a good night's sleep, and she nodded wordlessly before leaving the room. She stiffened as she saw Rafe leaning back against the wall outside, the palms of her hands at once feeling damp. 'I—er—Rosemary is sitting with Robert——'

'I know.' He straightened, his warm gaze never leaving hers. 'I asked her to.'

'Oh.' She frowned. 'Er—Do you know which bedroom I'm to use? Rosemary said——'

'Yes, I know.' He took her arm in a firm grasp, keeping her at his side as they walked down the hallway, stopping to push open one of the doors.

Brooke held back. 'This is your room——'

'Yes.'

'No!' She gave him a panicked look, feeling herself pulled unresistingly into the green and cream room.

'Yes, my darling Brooke,' he smiled at her gently, all harshness gone from him, his eyes a warm liquid grey. 'Yes,' he repeated huskily, closing the door on the outside world.

CHAPTER SEVEN

BROOKE looked up at him in the glow from the single lamp on his bedside table, knowing she couldn't allow this to happen, that Rafe must never be allowed to make love to her. She would be too easily recognisable as Jacqui under the cover of darkness, the hands and senses working independent of sight, and Rafe must surely remember the body of the woman who had been his wife. Admittedly they had only been together a short time before her body began to change with the growth of their child, but even so she couldn't take the risk.

Did she *want* to? Her physical response to Rafe was something she was learning she had little control over. And he didn't seem to be able control his response to her either. She had to leave the intimacy of this room!

She looked up at him with clear blue eyes. 'I would prefer to sleep in the spare room,' she told him distantly.

His mouth quirked into a mocking smile. 'I don't intend for you to "sleep" anywhere for some time,' he drawled.

'Rafe——'

'Brooke,' he taunted, moving steadily towards her as he easily held her immobile with his gaze. 'Darling, this isn't wrong,' his voice softened coaxingly as he gently clasped her shoulders to draw her against him. 'I want you so much,' he spoke into the perfumed softness of her hair. 'I want to give you so much.'

She stiffened. 'I don't want anything from you,' she snapped. 'If I ever gave myself to you it wouldn't be because I expected the expensive presents I'm sure your other mistresses demand,' she glared at him furiously.

Rafe smoothed the frown from between her eyes with gentle fingertips, smiling warmly. 'I don't want you as a mistress, Brooke,' he said gently. 'That gives the impression of subservience, and you've made it clear from the beginning that we meet as equals. I want you as a lover, Brooke,' he explained softly. 'I want to share things with you, be with you as much as possible, I want to learn to *know* you.'

She felt a brief moment of pain that he could offer Brooke Adamson, a woman he barely knew, all the things he should have given her as his wife. He had never shared anything but physical love with Jacqui, had spent only the evenings he wasn't working with her, and from the lies he had thought about her he had certainly never learnt to know her. But she could tell by the sincerity of his expression that he meant what he said, that he really wanted that closeness with Brooke Adamson.

It was an invitation she found hard to resist, and she swayed towards him, her head on his chest.

His arms tightened convulsively before he held her away from him. 'Now I'll take you to the bedroom you're to use for the night.'

For a moment her eyes widened in bewilderment at this rejection of her, fearing some cruel game, then she saw the lines etched beside Rafe's mouth, the strain in his eyes, and she knew that he didn't really want her to leave, that he was just giving her what he thought she wanted. And with sudden clarity she knew that it wasn't what she wanted at all, that she wanted to be here with him for this one night at least.

'The bed in here looks quite comfortable,' she told him lightly.

'It is. But I—I'm trying to give you time, Brooke,' he said in a strangulated voice.

She looked at him beneath lowered lashes. 'And if I don't want time, if I just want you?'

He swallowed hard. 'I'm here any time you need me.'

'Now?'

'Yes!'

She moved back into his arms, and their lips met in a volcanic kiss, all thoughts other than pleasing each other fleeing from their minds.

Four years ago Brooke had still been a child, both mentally and physically, but these long years had given her a new maturity, and with that maturity came a physical knowledge of Rafe she had never realised before. Within seconds they were both naked on the bed, and with a daring she had once thought herself incapable of she explored the hard lines of his taut body, hearing the ragged tempo of his breathing as her lips closed on his warm flesh. She felt him shudder beneath her, knew he was fast spiralling to the heights where nothing mattered but the wild caresses of her hands and lips across his body.

He relaxed slightly as she moved up his body to kiss his sweat-dampened chest, although not for long, gasping as she touched the hardened male nipples with the tip of her moist tongue.

'No more,' he groaned, drawing her on top of him to frame her passion-flushed face with trembling hands. 'I want to be gentle with you, Brooke,' his voice rasped huskily with desire. 'I wanted to take my time, but I find I can't.' He looked at her searchingly. 'I need you now, darling, if I'm not to——'

Her fingertips on his lips halted further speech, knowing what it had cost him to admit this complete lack of control. 'Next time you can be gentle,' she assured him. 'Next time you can take it slower. But I need you too now. *Please*!'

With a heartfelt groan he moved to pin her to the bed beneath him, his hair dark against her creamy skin as his tongue and teeth caressed the throbbing peaks of her breasts.

'*Now*, Rafe!' she encouraged heatedly, her body on fire for him.

He nudged her legs apart with one of his own, moving between her parted thighs, lowering himself down on her as he gently possessed her, filling her, warming her, until she didn't know where his body began and hers finished. Then he began to move deeply inside her, long languorous thrusts that sent pleasure surging through her body, and her legs wrapped about his as he brought her body up to meet and match each thrust.

Brooke felt the heat spreading through her body, felt the euphoria claim her to the tips of her hands and feet, knowing Rafe had reached the summit with her as he shuddered into her with a ragged groan, their bodies still shaking as the aftermath of their mutual climax racked through their joined bodies.

'I'm too heavy for you.' He moved away from her, groaning as another spasm of pleasure shot through him as he moved apart from her, falling back on the bed at her side to stare up at the ceiling, his body glistening with sweat.

Her breathing was slow to steady, and when she glanced at Rafe it was to see him still staring sightlessly up at the ceiling. What had just happened between them had been truly beautiful, but could it possibly have told him that his wife wasn't dead after all, that the woman lying at his side was in fact she? God, had her moment of weakness robbed her of all she had sought to keep the last three years?

'Brooke!' With a rasped cry he turned to bury his face against her breasts, his arms tight about her.

He certainly didn't know her as the wife he had hated, but what could be wrong with him? 'Rafe?' She tried to see his face, to see if his harsh features could tell her anything about his strange behaviour. 'What is it?' she demanded anxiously. 'Did I do something wrong?'

'No, nothing,' he groaned, his breath warm against her skin. 'Was that as wonderful for you as it was for me?'

'Yes,' she answered without hesitation.

'Jacqui and I had a very good physical—No, please don't move away from me!' He moved to lean on his elbow, looking down at her, his dark hair completely ruffled, making him look younger, more vulnerable somehow. 'I'm trying to explain why just now, for a fleeting moment, I felt almost guilty that I could have enjoyed you as much as I did.' He smoothed her hair from her damp brow. 'I always thought there could never be another woman alive who gave me the satisfaction she could,' he continued remorselessly. 'But you just did.'

'Rafe——'

'Towards the end of my marriage I used to leave her bed disgusted with myself for taking what she no longer wanted to give,' he seemed to be speaking almost to himself, refocusing on her with effort. 'You're a generous lover, Brooke. You must have been very happy with your husband.'

'Like you with your wife, at first,' she answered stiffly, knowing he was right about her reluctance to share his bed towards the end of their marriage—she had been too frightened of the deterioration of their relationship by then to be able to respond to him completely. 'The reality of living with someone all the time is much less glamorous than it at first appears, especially when there's a wedding ring involved,' she added tightly.

'You don't ever want to marry again?'

'Never!' she shuddered.

'But you'll be my lover?' He tensed as she avoided his gaze. 'Brooke?' He wrenched her face round to look at him, uncertainty reflected in his eyes. 'I won't let you escape me now,' he vowed firmly. 'You're mine!'

He didn't seem to notice her lack of reply as he ruthlessly plundered her mouth, relentlessly punishing her for daring to frighten him in that way.

Their second coming together was slower, longer, but no less intense, both of them falling asleep only to wake again a short time later to make love for a third time.

'I can't seem to get enough of you,' Rafe murmured against her breast. 'It's as if you might fade away from me in the morning and I'll never again know the beauty of your body.' His eyes were almost black as he looked at her in dawn's early light. 'You won't leave me, will you, Brooke?'

'I won't leave,' she replied, and he seemed satisfied with her answer. But even as his lips claimed her again, she knew that she would assuredly stop being Rafe's lover as soon as she left this bed in a few hours' time, that tonight must never be repeated even though she would remain in the cottage on the Charlwood estate.

Rafe was still sleeping as she dressed quietly the next morning, not even stirring as she let herself out of the room. His total exhaustion wasn't surprising; he had flown from Australia the previous day, and then made love to her all night. She felt relieved that she had been able to leave his side without further questioning from him, knowing instinctively that he wasn't going to like any of the answers she was prepared to give him.

She had to have been mad to give in to her impulse like that; she could so easily have ruined her life for a second time if Rafe had once realised who she was. She had no excuse even to herself for what had happened, she just didn't have any defences against Rafe's need of her. But she would have to be stronger from now on; she knew that Rafe would be all the more determined now that they had spent one night together.

Connie was sitting beside the bed reading Robert a Noddy story when she entered the nursery, and turned to give Brooke a friendly smile. 'Feeling better?'

Brooke still couldn't get over this change in the other girl, she didn't know if she ever would! As for feeling better, she wondered what Rafe's staff would say if they knew she had spent the night in his bed being made thorough love to!

'Have you been poorly too?' Robert asked from the bed—a much improved Robert, although he was obviously still not well, the fever having left his face pale and his eyes heavy.

'She's been taking care of you.' Connie ruffled his hair affectionately and stood up. 'I was just about to get Robert some breakfast,' she told Brooke. 'Would you like me to bring you some too?'

The possibility of having to sit down to breakfast with Rafe after the night of passion they had just shared wasn't something she wanted right now. 'What are you having, Robert?' she asked lightly.

'Scrambled egg,' he replied instantly. 'And bread and butter.'

'A lot better, I see,' she shared a smile with Connie. 'I'll have the same, if you're sure you don't mind? I could go down and get it——'

'I really don't mind,' Connie said almost shyly.

Robert managed to eat very little of the fluffy golden eggs, but the fact that he had eaten a little, drunk a little milk, was a vast improvement on the last two days.

Brooke was helping Nanny Perkins make up a clean bed for him when the nursery door opened behind her, knowing instinctively that it was Rafe even before the other woman excused herself and quietly left the room.

'Daddy!' Robert cried excitedly, having slept through the time his father had sat with him the previous evening, and so not having been aware of his return.

Rafe swung him up in his arms, continuing to hold him as the tiny arms clung about his neck. 'I think you've been having everyone running round for nothing,' his father teased him. 'You don't look ill to me.'

'But I was,' Robert protested with all the indignation of the very young. 'Wasn't I, Brooke?'

The question forced her to look at the man and the boy, studiously avoiding the intensity of dark grey eyes, knowing Rafe was trying to read something of her thoughts from her face. She deliberately kept her expression bland, although that didn't stop her being aware of how attractive Rafe looked in the black silk shirt and light grey trousers, his dark hair still damp from the shower he had taken, his jaw freshly shaved, smelling lightly of aftershave and soap. Her own skin had smelt slightly of that same aftershave when she left his arms this morning, and a blush came unbidden to her cheeks.

'Yes, you were,' her voice sounded brittle as she answered Robert. 'Although you're a lot better now.'

Rafe put his son down on the newly made bed. 'Thanks to Brooke taking care of you,' he said gravely. 'We both have a lot to thank her for.' As he straightened he turned suddenly and caught her gaze with his, eyes warm and caressing.

'I——' she broke off as the door opened, turning to see Nanny Perkins standing in the doorway.

'Oh, I'm sorry.' The older woman looked uncomfortable. 'I thought you'd both gone. I was just going to give Robert a wash—I'll come back later.'

'No,' Rafe stopped her, crossing the room to grasp Brooke's elbow. 'Miss Adamson and I were just going down to have breakfast. We'll be back before you know it,' he assured his son indulgently.

'I ate earlier with Robert,' Brooke refused, her arm tingling where he touched her.

He looked down at her with steady grey eyes. 'Then sit with me while I have mine,' he encouraged throatily. 'I'm sure you'd like another cup of coffee.'

'I——'

'Please, Brooke.'

Her lashes fluttered nervously at the pleading in his voice, and she looked awkwardly at Nanny Perkins. The older woman was making a point of taking Robert's clean clothing out of the drawers, giving every impression of not hearing their conversation, or the intensity of her employer as he asked the previously resented Miss Adamson to join him downstairs. And perhaps she didn't hear, Brooke thought ruefully, perhaps it was just her own imagination that had made it seem Rafe wanted her with him so badly.

'Very well,' she gave an inclination of her head, bending to kiss Robert before following Rafe from the room. Her tension returned tenfold as she found herself alone with him in the hallway, and she stiffened as he turned to pull her into his arms.

'When I woke up half an hour ago,' he spoke into her hair, talking softly, 'I thought I must have dreamt you. But I didn't, did I?'

Brooke didn't know how to answer him, not wanting to be in his arms like this, knowing she had to keep to the resolve she had made last night, that she couldn't allow her physical weakness towards this man to continue. 'I don't know what you mean, Mr Charlwood.' She tried to pull away from him, but he only laughed softly, his arms tightening about her.

'You know, Brooke,' he teased gently. 'It was as beautiful for you as it was for me.'

'I——' Rafe's mouth softly possessing hers prevented further speech, his hands on her spine moulding her to him as her body arched into his of its own volition.

She didn't want this, knew she should stop it. And yet she couldn't, and her arms went up about his neck as she curled her fingers in the dark hair at his nape, deepening the kiss as her lips parted fully to his, the tip of his tongue running along the sensitive inner skin of her mouth.

'No, I didn't dream a thing,' he rested his forehead on hers minutes later, his breathing soft and uneven. 'Brooke, you don't regret what happened between us last night?' he frowned as her expression remained pensive.

Did she regret it? If she were honest with herself, and since her break-up with Rafe three years ago she had tried to be that, the answer was no. Last night had shown her a Rafe she had never seen before, a Rafe who made her feel like a woman instead of a child, a man who had shown her tenderness and giving rather than just possession. No, in all honesty, she couldn't regret last night. But she couldn't put herself in the position again where she would be dependent upon Rafe for anything, especially not physical or emotional love. If she did he would destroy her a second time as surely as he had the first.

'No,' she answered truthfully.

'Good,' he grinned, a boyishly relaxed Rafe who seemed almost like a stranger to her after the coldly aloof man she had known in the past, his arm about her shoulders now as they walked down the stairs together.

'You?' she asked stiffly.

'I don't regret a thing,' he still smiled. 'You've made me feel free, free to feel again, to want again, to——'

'I'm glad,' she interrupted sharply, not wanting him to say any more. She had believed he loved her once before and it had turned out to be only a shallow emotion. She didn't want to hear that word mentioned between them this time. 'Physically we're—compatible,' she added, determined he would know that was all it had been to her.

'Brooke——'

'What would you like for your breakfast?' she asked him brightly, forcing a mischievous smile to her lips as they entered the dining-room. 'Sit down here,' she made a point of seeing him seated at the table, meeting his laughing grey eyes. 'I'll serve you,' she moved to the array of dishes keeping the food warm. 'Bacon, sausages, eggs,' she turned to look at him teasingly. 'And of course, kidneys.'

He grimaced at the latter. 'You were doing so well until you got to the kidneys,' he drawled. 'Make it tomatoes instead and I'll take it.'

She had known his dislike of kidneys, had deliberately suggested them to allay his suspicions; she had been doing *too* well, knowing his preferences in food as she knew his preference in bed, preferences she had used as if by instinct during their night together. 'Here you are,' she put the plate in front of him, evading his grasp to sit across the table from him, pouring them both a cup of coffee.

Rafe smiled at her, seeming to find it difficult to stop staring at her.

'Your food is getting cold,' she finally had to prompt him, confused by his gaze fixed on her.

He grasped her hand across the table. 'I don't give a damn about the food. Brooke, I——'

'Rafe—Oh,' Rosemary came to an abrupt halt in the doorway, looking at them both in confusion. 'I didn't realise—I'll come back when you've finished.'

'No!' Brooke released her hand, standing up to go to the other woman. 'Come and join Rafe, I have to be going now anyway. Yes, I do,' she insisted firmly as she could see he was about to protest. 'I haven't been home for some time.'

His mouth firmed. 'At least finish your coffee.'

This Rafe she could understand, the Rafe who hated to be thwarted. And Brooke Adamson had no reason, no reason at all to give him anything he wanted, not even such a small request at this. 'Only if Rosemary will join us,' she gave him a tight smile before turning to the woman at her side. 'Will you?' she prompted gently.

Rosemary looked upset, and Brooke had an idea it

might have something to do with Patrick's non-appearance this morning. Although the other woman would be too proud to say so.

'If you're wondering where Patrick is,' Rafe seemed to guess his sister-in-law's dilemma, 'he's gone away for a few days on business for me.'

Rosemary seemed to stiffen. 'And why should I be interested in your brother's whereabouts, Rafe?' she drawled dismissively. 'I'm sure it hasn't escaped your notice, but we're separated.'

'You're simply living apart for the moment,' he corrected. 'You can hardly be separated when this is Patrick's home.'

Green eyes flashed angrily. 'Are you asking me to leave, Rafe?' she snapped.

'Don't be childish, Rosemary,' he sighed. 'I merely think the situation between Patrick and yourself is a little ridiculous.'

'Indeed?' Two bright red spots of angry colour heightened Rosemary's cheeks. 'And I suppose your behaviour over Jacqui wasn't ridiculous?' she derided bitchily.

Rafe's eyes grew suddenly cold, his body still. 'I don't think this is the time or the place to discuss my wife,' he bit the words out through barely moving lips, his tone telling Rosemary it would be dangerous to goad him any further.

All Rosemary's haughtiness seemed to disintegrate in that moment, and with a choked cry she ran from the room.

'Leave her!' Rafe instructed Brooke tautly as she would have followed the other woman from the room.

She turned with indignantly widened eyes, breathing slowly. 'What did you say?' she asked in a controlled voice.

'Brooke——'

'I won't be ordered about by you or anyone else, *Mr*

Charlwood,' she told him in a cold voice. 'There appear to be plenty of servants in the house if you want to act the overlord,' she continued abruptly. 'But *I* am not one of them.' She turned to leave, then felt herself pulled back against a hard masculine body before she had got very far.

'I'm sorry, Brooke,' Rafe spoke against her temple. 'I'm sorry,' his hands caressed the length of her arms as he held her back against him. 'I think I'm too used to giving out orders,' he added ruefully. 'Forgive me?'

She swallowed hard, weakening at his close proximity and repentant manner, knowing he had once again defeated her intention of putting them back on the footing of enemies. 'Forgiven,' she said huskily.

He turned her in his arms, moulding her body to his. 'I just think Patrick and Rosemary need to sort out their own problems.'

'But you've sent him away,' she shrugged.

He nodded. 'Only for a few days at the most. I doubt that will make much difference to their situation.'

She knew he was right. The hostility between the other couple had been going on for weeks now, a couple more days couldn't make that much difference. 'What did—What did Rosemary mean about your wife?' She absently played with a button on his shirt, her head going back as she sensed his sudden reserve. 'Or would you rather not talk about her?'

He shrugged. 'I have no objection to talking about her—to you. Although I don't think now is the right time to discuss anything so personal,' he smiled down at her to take the sting out of his words. 'Robert will be wondering what's keeping us.'

'You really love him, don't you?' she realised with a frown, wondering now how she could ever have doubted it. No uncaring father would come all the way back from Australia to be with his sick child.

'Why should you have the impression that I didn't?

Ah,' he nodded, smiling slightly. 'Aunt Jocelyn was a dear, but I'm afraid she didn't understand my feelings for either Jacqui or Robert. She was the one who gave you the impression I neglect my son, wasn't she?' he gave a rueful sigh as she blushed. 'I know I'm away a lot on business, and perhaps I needn't make some of those trips myself,' he spoke quietly. 'But sometimes I have to get away from Charlwood, the memories this place holds for me. I'm not leaving Robert,' he explained gently. 'Sometimes the memories here crowd in on me and I have to get away and be alone for a while. Can you understand that?'

She could more than understand it, she felt the same way about this house herself. She had become a pale ghost of a woman here, had lived in Rafe's shadow until she had no personality of her own. And he seemed to think last night gave him the right to do that to her for a second time. She would *never* become his slave again, a woman almost afraid to move for fear of angering him in some incomprehensible way.

'I can understand that,' she nodded, moving away from him. 'But you'll have to go back up to Robert on your own, I'm afraid. I haven't been back to the cottage for two days,' she insisted as he would have protested. 'Robert is a lot better now, and he has you with him.'

'I doubt he'll appreciate that,' Rafe grimaced.

'You'll persuade him,' she smiled tightly, knowing herself how persuasive he could be. 'I'd like to go home and have a long leisurely bath, and then maybe catch up on a few hours' sleep.'

'That sounds like a good idea.'

Her mouth quirked at his suggestive tone. '*You* happen to be the reason I need this extra sleep,' she mocked.

'Me?' He feigned innocence.

Brooke felt her breath catch in her throat. This Rafe really was too easy to like, to fall in love with; he was the Rafe of their first meeting, of their first two weeks together. And she would have to harden her heart towards him; she could not fall under his spell a second time.

'Yes, you,' she said abruptly. 'Tell Robert I'll be back to see him this afternoon.' She moved to the door.

'And me?'

She turned slowly at the softly spoken question. 'I'm sure I'll see you this afternoon too.'

'I'm sorry to interrupt, Mr Charlwood,' a hesitant Connie stood in the doorway, 'but Robert is getting a little fretful for you both.'

Brooke looked back at Rafe. 'Explain to him for me, will you,' she said lightly. 'I really do have to go,' and she left before he could make any objections, hurrying from the house as if a pack of wolves were at her heels.

The cottage seemed like a sanctuary to her, a cool untroubled sanctuary where she could even forget that last night had happened, could think of it as just a bad dream. If only it had been bad! It had been a time apart, just a man and a woman who wanted each other badly.

A long soak in the bath relaxed her enough for her to feel able to sleep, and she pulled the bedroom curtains against the world, forcing her mind not to allow her the luxury of thought, knowing that if she did she would never sleep.

She slept until late afternoon, and showered when she woke up, feeling utterly revived once she had washed and blow-dried her hair, dressing in a turquoise silk dress with a navy blue tie-belt before walking back to the house, the warm sunshine lifting her spirits. She felt even happier when she learnt that Rafe was in his study taking business calls while Robert had a nap. She was to be spared another confrontation for now!

She could see for herself that Robert was a lot better now, sleeping deeply, his colour almost back to normal.

Nanny Perkins told her the doctor was very pleased with his progress. That the nanny and Connie still seemed to be accepting her she felt grateful for.

Once Robert woke up they played Snap together, then Brooke read to him as he began to tire again, joining him for his afternoon tea before leaving him to Nanny Perkins to settle down for the night, aware that she had intruded on the other woman's territory long enough.

She had seen nothing of Rafe during her visit, although she knew he had spent most of the day with Robert, only leaving his side once he had fallen asleep. Her breath left her with a sigh as she once again managed to leave the house without protest.

But she was sensitive to every noise she heard outside the cottage that evening, expecting Rafe to turn up at any moment, sure that she hadn't seen the last of him for today, knowing he still believed them to be lovers.

But by ten o'clock she felt relatively safe from confrontation tonight, and she was in the process of turning off the lights to go up to bed when a sharp knock sounded on the door. Rafe! It had to be him. She tensed for what she knew was going to be an unpleasant meeting.

As soon as she opened the door she was swept up into strong arms, held tightly against Rafe's chest as he kissed her hungrily. Every thought fled from her mind except kissing him back, feeling herself melting against him, becoming part of him.

She *was* a part of him, a part that she now knew would never end. She still loved this man—despite everything, she still loved Rafe!

CHAPTER EIGHT

Rafe picked her up in his arms, swinging her up against his chest to stride inside the cottage, kicking the door shut with his foot before carrying her up the stairs to her bedroom.

Brooke gazed up at his hard profile with stunned eyes, knowing she was as powerless now as she had been in the past, now that she had mentally admitted the love she still had for the man who was her husband. She was a prisoner again, a prisoner of her own love, had no way out of this madness now.

Rafe sat down on the bed, still holding her in his arms, looking down at her with warm grey eyes. 'Did you think I wasn't coming?' he asked huskily.

'Yes,' she answered truthfully.

His long hand curved about her burning cheek. 'I spent the evening sitting with Robert—he's asleep now. Why didn't you come and see me when you came back to the house this afternoon?'

She was taken aback by the question, and she blinked rapidly. 'You were busy——'

'I'll never be too busy for you, Brooke.' His arms tightened about her. 'Did you get some rest this afternoon?'

She nodded her answer. 'Did you rest too?'

He gave a husky laugh of pleasure. 'The thought of being with you again has more than kept me awake.'

'Rafe—Oh, *Rafe*!' Her protest became a groan of capitulation as his hand moved down her throat and into the vee-neckline of her dress to curve possessively about her warm breast. Her hands moved across his chest and about his neck as she pulled his head down to hers, almost drowning in the deep grey warmth of his eyes before their mouths moved together in mounting passion.

'You're mine!' he grated as his lips moved moistly down her throat.

'Yes.' She gave herself up to the inevitable at that moment. It seemed she was once again his, for as long—or short—a time as he wanted her. And for the moment he wanted her very much, wanted Brooke Adamson. And she would remain Brooke Adamson to him; she would never let him know she was his wife. As Brooke Adamson she could continue to live in the cottage once their affair was over—and this time she was prepared for the fact that it *would* one day end.

His thumbtip moved caressingly over her hardened nipple, pleasure invading every particle of her body as he smoothed the material away from her breast to claim the throbbing tip with moist lips, loving the sensitive nipple with a moist tongue as he bit down with gentle eroticism.

Her dress fell away from her body with the minimum of effort, her underclothes quickly following. Tonight Rafe couldn't wait for her to help him undress, but threw his clothes haphazardly to the floor before joining her on the bed. Their hunger for each other hadn't abated during their previous night together, and what should have been a slow and languorous loving became a heated explosion, their sweat-dampened bodies clinging together in total exhaustion afterwards.

Rafe's head lay against her breasts as he caressed her trembling body from the shuddering aftermath of their passion. 'The first time with you always seems to be out of my control,' he spoke ruefully.

'*First* time?' she teased languorously, the whole of her body one pleasurable ache.

As he raised his head to look at her she could see the desire already rekindling in his eyes. 'Every time I look at you I want to make love to you, and if I did that I could be dead within the week!' He grinned, suddenly looking younger. 'I can't think of a more pleasurable way to go!'

'Rafe!' she giggled into the hard warmth of his chest, raising anxious eyes as she sensed him tense. 'What is it?' She searched the stillness of his face, terrified that she had somehow alerted him to her true identity. She had even more to lose than Robert now; she knew that even though this new relationship with Rafe would only be temporary, that she didn't want it to end yet. 'Rafe?' she prompted worriedly.

He touched the parted softness of her mouth. 'That's the first time I've ever heard you really laugh,' he explained softly. 'It was beautiful.'

She relaxed as she smiled. 'I laughed because I'm happy. And I'm happy because you just made wonderful love to me.'

His kissed her lingeringly on the lips. 'No more wonderful than you did to me.' His gaze was intent. 'You didn't want me to come here tonight, did you?'

She blushed at the directness of the question, making a show of getting beneath the bedclothes while she thought how to answer him. 'Let's snuggle up together.' She put her arms about him as they lay together beneath the blankets; the nights were becoming chill as summer drew to an end.

'Brooke,' Rafe prompted softly against her throat.

She swallowed hard, knowing he must be aware of the nervous movement. 'I don't quite understand what you want from me, from any relationship we have,' she admitted throatily. 'We began as enemies, and now I don't know what we are.'

'We're lovers, darling,' his hand rested possessively on her hip, 'and all I want from the relationship is you.'

'You won't—demand anything I don't want to give?'

'Such as?'

'Such as—permanence, commitment.'

'You can't give me those things?'

'No,' she replied unhesitantly.

'Then I won't ask for them.'

She chewed on her inner lip. 'You're sure this will be enough for you?'

Rafe moved to look down at her. 'I'm sure of only one thing at the moment—that I want you, to be with you, any way you'll let me.'

'It will work both ways,' she told him, anxious he should understand. 'I won't ask anything of you either, not permanence or commitment, and certainly not fidelity.'

'My fidelity to you is something you need never question,' his arms tightened painfully about her, 'because I intend to spend every night here with you from now on.'

'Here?' she repeated dazedly.

He nodded. 'Unless you would consent to move up to the main house with me?'

'No!' Brooke could hardly contain her shudder at the thought. 'But I—What will everyone say?'

'If by everyone you mean the family and staff then I don't really give a damn what they say or think,' he dismissed with some of his normal arrogance. 'This is where I want to be.'

'And—and Robert?' Somehow the thought of their son knowing the full intimacy of their relationship was distasteful to her.

'Robert is a different matter,' Rafe seemed to agree with her. 'He just wouldn't understand. I'm not sure that we do yet,' he added ruefully.

'Isn't it enough to accept and enjoy what we do have?'

'God, yes,' he agreed deeply, kissing her with renewed desire, passion soon flaring out of control to blaze though every particle of their bodies.

They slept deeply in each other's arms, and Brooke woke at last with a start of surprise as Rafe left her. 'Wha—What is it?' she asked groggily. 'What's happening?' She came more fully awake to find Rafe standing next to the bed.

He bent and kissed her comfortingly on the forehead, tucking the bedclothes more firmly about her. 'It's only the telephone, darling,' he soothed. 'I've been expecting a call; I'll take it downstairs.'

She blinked the sleep from her eyes, having trouble focusing on him. 'What time is it?' It was still dark outside, that much she could see!

'Three o'clock.' He smiled down at her. 'Now go back to sleep. If you're still awake when I come back to bed consider your sleep over for the night,' he warned sensuously before leaving the room. The ringing of the extension on her bedside table stopped as Rafe picked the telephone up downstairs, and she heard the faint murmur of his voice as he spoke to his caller.

Who on earth could be calling him this time of night? And how had they known he could be reached at *her* cottage? The answer to the latter was a little unsettling, banishing all thought of sleep from her mind.

Rafe's conversation with his caller went on for some time, but finally the extension in the bedroom gave a slight pinging noise as the receiver was replaced downstairs. And still Rafe didn't come back to bed.

Brooke got out of bed to pull on her silky robe, knowing by the amount of clothes still lying on the floor that Rafe only wore black fitted trousers. He was sitting in the chair beside the telephone in the lounge; the room was in total darkness, illuminated only by the light flooding in from the open doorway to the hall behind Brooke.

'No!' he rasped as she would have put on one of the lamps.

She frowned her puzzlement with his strange

behaviour, walking across the room to his side, unconsciously provocative with the light shining through her robe, kneeling in front of him as his attention seemed to be locked in space. 'Rafe?' she touched his hand gently. 'Is there anything wrong? What was the call about?' It no longer bothered her how the caller had got this number, her concern was all for Rafe, a strangely haggard Rafe.

He was very pale, grey almost, his eyes almost black, a slight trembling to his hands as he pushed the ruffled dark hair from his brow.

'It isn't Robert, is it?' she questioned sharply at his continued silence.

His breath left him in a ragged sigh. 'No,' his voice was gruff, 'It isn't Robert.' His gaze finally lifted to hers, and she was stunned by the pain she saw in his eyes.

'Darling, what is it?' she groaned her concern for him, sitting on the arm of his chair to pull him into her arms. 'Tell me. Let me help you.'

'No one can help me,' came his choked reply as his arms moved convulsively about her. 'Oh, Brooke, I— I——'

'What is it?' Desperation sharpened her voice as she heard the utter despair in his tone. 'For God's sake tell me,' she pleaded. 'I can't bear to see you hurting like this.'

He looked up at her with jet-black eyes. 'Take me back to bed,' he pleaded huskily. 'Let me love you.'

She didn't hesitate, and the two of them went back upstairs to lose themselves in each other's arms. If this was the only way she could help him she would willingly do so, knowing that there were still a lot of barriers between them, that Rafe would always find it difficult to confide that he had worries and disappointments like other human beings.

She lay in bed the next morning at seven-thirty

watching him dress, a smile of absolute contentment on
her face. Rafe still looked pale and drawn, but
considering that he had spent the remainder of the night
making exquisite love to her that wasn't surprising. Her
body ached from the unaccustomed pleasure she had
known time and time again during the night, although
somehow she didn't feel tired, just satiated.

Rafe came to sit on the side of the bed, a hand on the
pillow either side of her head as he bent over her, fully
dressed now, his hair combed neatly into place. 'What
are you going to do today?'

She stretched contentedly, her arms going up about
his neck as her fingers became entangled with the hair
at his nape, completely confident of her role as Brooke
Adamson, his mistress. 'After last night?' she teased
throatily. 'I'm going to sleep, of course! Actually,' she
laughed happily as an indulgent smile lightened his
austere features, 'I thought I might spend the day with
Robert. And then tonight I might prepare dinner for an
insatiable man I know!' The last was said questioningly;
she was still not too sure of Rafe, remembering from
the past how he could turn into a growling stranger.
But she was determined not to be the cowering Jacqui
Charlwood, she wanted to be the equal he had claimed
Brooke Adamson to be.

'If that's me then I accept.' He bent to kiss her on the
nose.

She smiled up at him. 'What other insatiable men do
I know?' Her smile instantly froze on her lips, knowing
the incredible possessiveness Rafe could display.

To her relief he continued to smile, not a shadow of
anger in his eyes. 'None.' He bent to kiss her briefly,
lifting his head only to return to her mouth with a
hunger that told of his renewed desire.

'You have to go to work,' she chided softly as he
nibbled on her earlobe.

'Do I?' he muttered. 'I have three years of loving to

make up for, and I can't think of any other woman I would rather be with than you.'

Once again she was reminded that as his wife she had disillusioned him against women. But she was also the woman who had set him free of that, so surely she could take what he so freely gave now—his desire. 'I want you too, Rafe,' she told him softly, her arms tightening about his neck.

'Do you?' he moaned against her breast, the movements of his tongue making the tip hard and sensitive.

'You know I do,' she groaned her weakness as he lay on the bed beside her, all thought of Rafe going to work completely forgotten by both of them.

'Would you spend the day with me?' He held her against his shoulder a long time later.

Her fingers were entwined in the wiry dampness of the hair on his tanned chest. 'Don't you have to go to work?'

'Not if I can spend the day with you.'

He sounded so relaxed, more so than she had ever heard him before, his worry of last night completely evaporated. And she felt happy too, knew that they really were equals this time around, that Rafe was no more sure of her than she was of him. And that was the way he had to stay; he must never know she had been stupid enough to fall in love with him again. He had to believe that her interest was the same as his, purely physical.

She squirmed against him with sensual abandon. 'Here?' she said throatily.

'No, not here.' Laughing softly, he put her away from him, getting out of the bed with a languid stretch of his naked body. 'I want to last out the week,' he bent to gently slap her bare bottom. 'I don't think I've made love this much in thirty-six hours since I was in my impetuous youth. And it was never this good then. You do things to me, Brooke Adamson, that make it impossible for me to leave you.'

'I do?' she teased, leaning across the bed to run her fingertips up his leg and along his hardening thigh. 'I thought we were going to spend the day together,' she pouted as he moved away from her to begin dressing. 'I think we should do something we'll both enjoy, don't you?'

He zipped up his trousers, pulling on his shirt. 'That's what we will be doing, we're going to spend the day with Robert.'

All teasing left her at the thought of her son, and she fell back against the pillows. 'I'll join you over at the house once I've dressed and had breakfast.'

'Brooke?' Rafe came back to sit on the side of he bed.

'Oh no, you don't,' she laughingly pushed him off. 'The last time you did that we wasted a whole hour——'

'Wasted?' He sounded outraged, coming towards her with mock anger. 'I'll show you how wasted it was!' he threatened with determination.

With a teasing laugh she jumped out of the bed and ran into the adjoining bathroom, locking the door behind her as she knew he followed her.

'I'll deal with you later tonight,' he threatened softly against the closed door.

'If I don't deal with you first,' she mocked.

'We'll see,' he laughed softly, and a few seconds later he could be heard moving lightly down the stairs, the front door closing soon afterwards.

Brooke turned to lean back against the door, her eyes widening in wonder as she caught sight of her reflection in the bathroom mirror. She knew, in all modesty, that she had never looked so beautiful. She had never felt so beautiful before either. Even during her first two weeks with Rafe, at the apartment in London, she hadn't felt this happy and contented. She could be contented as Rafe's mistress, knew that when it ended she would surely be hurt, but that she wouldn't lose Robert this time too.

Their day with their son was the happiest Brooke had ever known, so much so that she could almost believe they were a normal family. In fact, she almost forgot they weren't as she and Rafe amused a Robert becoming impatient with the way he still felt so tired, not at all pleased with the fact that he was pressed into taking a nap after they had all shared lunch together in the nursery,

Rafe's arm was about her waist as they left the room. 'A nap sounds like a good idea,' he quirked a questioning eyebrow.

Her mouth curved in amusement. 'I have to think of your health,' she shook her head. 'After all, you're a lot older than me, and——' she was prevented from further speech as he pushed her into his bedroom and proceeded to show her that the difference in their ages made not the slightest difference to their stamina.

Brook lived in a state of euphoria for the next three days—and nights. Robert was a lot better now, spending most of his time with her at the cottage, and Rafe came to her in the evenings as soon as he had showered and changed, staying until morning when he would leave her with a reluctance that warmed her all day.

She prepared him a roast dinner on their fourth evening together, pleased that he enjoyed her cooking. Living at Charlwood as they had in the past she had never had the opportunity to provide these sort of homely comforts for him, having to fit into his lifestyle then, and she was enjoying caring for him as much as he seemed to enjoy having it done for him.

'I saw Rosemary briefly today,' she told him casually

as she served their dessert, an apple Charlotte, something she knew he was very fond of.

His eyes narrowed. 'Yes?'

'She still looks—very unhappy.'

'She is,' he sighed. 'Patrick is back in London, but he refuses to come back here.'

'You asked him to?' She couldn't hide her surprise, remembering his previous impatience with the situation between Rosemary and Patrick.

His expression softened. 'I did.' He gave a rueful smile. 'Maybe having found happiness again myself I'm trying to straighten everyone else out too,' he derided. 'I'm well aware of how misunderstandings can grow out of all proportion, how the longer a wound is left the worse it gets.' He was suddenly serious now. 'Jacqui and I had too many misunderstandings we were both too proud to discuss with each other.'

Brooke had stiffened at the mention of his wife. 'Oh, come on, Rafe,' she mocked lightly to ease her tension. 'Don't try and tell me you were one of those poor misunderstood husbands! I can't believe that,' she scorned.

'That wasn't what I said,' he answered quietly. 'I said Jacqui and I misunderstood *each other*.'

She moistened suddenly dry lips, interested in spite of herself. 'In what way?'

He shrugged. 'In every way, it seems. I loved her very much, you know.'

Her spoon slipped out of her hand on to the carpeted floor, and by the time she had taken it out to the kitchen and got herself a clean one in its place she had recovered her equilibrium enough to look at him without the revealing flush to her cheeks.

'I don't think she ever knew how much,' he added softly.

Brooke composed her features with effort. 'Really?' Her tone was stilted.

He picked restlessly at the dessert in his bowl, not really seeming to see it at all. 'You were right that night you said I was too set in my ways for marriage——'

'I didn't say that!' she gasped her objection, having lost her appetite for her dinner too.

Rafe's mouth twisted. 'My lifestyle was too established,' he amended dryly. 'It was,' he stated flatly. 'And I didn't see why a wife should change that. Oh, there were no other women,' he dismissed. 'Not once; I just didn't want anyone but her. I loved her so much, wanted her so much, I just didn't think of the fact that a wife would change my way of life.'

'Then why marry at all?' Brooke asked abruptly.

His hands clenched into fists. 'I wanted her to be mine. I thought my ring on her finger *made* her mine, body and soul.' His expression was harsh. 'She was so young, so—so——'

'Malleable?' she put in tensely.

'Yes!' he bit out. 'In my decision to make her so completely mine I forgot that she was a person in her own right. And in doing so I crushed everything I'd ever loved about her—her spirit, her beauty, and most of all her love for me. She did love me when we were first married,' he seemed to speak softly to himself, an almost lost look in his eyes.

Brooke didn't want to hear any more, she already knew all about how she had been destroyed by their marriage. She also knew Rafe had *never* loved her! 'Isn't this rather a strange conversation for us to be having?' she mocked dryly. 'I really have no wish to hear about your relationship with your wife, Rafe. Especially when she's been dead for nearly three years.'

'She'll never be dead to me.'

She raised startled lids. 'What do you mean?'

He looked at her with dull grey eyes. 'Every time I look at Robert I'm reminded of Jacqui.'

'Is that why——' she broke off, biting her bottom lip,

feeling guilty for what she had been about to say. Rafe loved his son, the way he had rushed back from Australia to be with him proved that.

'Why I often find it hard to be gentle with him?' Rafe finished dryly. 'Yes,' he sighed. 'Sometimes—sometimes I can see the way I hurt him without meaning to, I can see it in his eyes that are so like his mother's. They say the eyes are the mirrors of the soul; well, I know that by the time Jacqui left me that she *hated* me body and soul.'

'Oh, but——'

'Yes?' he demanded sharply.

'Surely she didn't leave you—you threw her out,' Brooke evaded looking at him.

'There was another man——'

'Greg Davieson.'

'Yes,' he said tautly. 'She went to him all the time—and there was nothing I could do to stop it.'

'You could have tried telling her you loved her,' Brooke told him bitterly. 'It might have helped.'

He sighed heavily. 'I never thought I needed to. I thought she understood how I felt.'

'She obviously didn't,' she snapped abruptly.

Rafe shook his head. 'I told you we had too many misunderstandings.'

'Well, that will never happen with us,' she dismissed lightly, standing up to clear the table. 'We know exactly where we stand.'

He turned to watch her. 'Do we?'

'Of course,' she kept her tone light. 'We enjoy being together, going to bed together, and neither of us wants any serious commitment.'

'Is that where we stand?' he asked slowly.

'You know it is.' Brooke walked over to put her arms down over his chest as she cuddled him from behind the chair. 'Now do you want to wash up—or go to bed?'

Rafe grinned at her teasing tone. 'Need you ask?'

'No,' she laughed huskily as she was swung up into his arms to be carried up the stairs to the bedroom. And as he made slow and tender love to her she was able to forget that even when she was his mistress he lied to her. All Rafe had ever felt for Jacqui was desire and a sense of possession, and it had been the latter that had been outraged when he thought her to be having an affair with Greg Davieson, not his love.

Rosemary brought Robert down to the cottage the next afternoon, and without consciously being aware of it Brooke tensed for the meeting. Living in the main house as she did Rosemary could hardly fail to notice the way Rafe disappeared to the cottage as soon as Robert had gone to bed in the evenings, or the fact that he arrived back at the house the next morning needing no breakfast and with only just enough time to spend a few minutes with Robert before changing and leaving for work. Brooke prepared herself for caustic comments from the other woman, and instead received a tentative smile that didn't quite reach pained green eyes.

'Would you like a cup of tea?' Brooke offered instantly, sensing the other woman's deep unhappiness, her need not to be alone.

'Thank you,' Rosemary accepted dully, seating herself at the kitchen table.

'Brooke, could I go outside in the garden, please?' Robert requested hopefully.

She smiled at her son, enjoying the afternoons they spent together now, someone from the house usually bringing him down for an hour or two, although this was the first time Rosemary had done so. 'Stay in the garden,' she warned, nodding her permission. 'You'll find your bucket and spade out there,' she opened the door for him. 'And don't dig up too many of the flowers!'

With a grin he dashed outside, digging happily in her flower-beds seconds later. She didn't hold out much hope for the flowers!

'You're very good with him,' Rosemary sighed, looking even more miserable. 'I don't have a clue.'

Brooke frowned at the other woman's desolation. 'He just wants love and attention. That's all most children want,' she added in a preoccupied voice.

'I've never learnt how to love them.' Rosemary's voice sharpened. 'Never had a lot to do with children, really. I can't have any of my own, you know.'

She did know, but as Jacqui, not as Brooke. 'A lot of women can't or don't have children nowadays,' she dismissed, putting the offered cup of tea in front of Rosemary before seating herself opposite the other woman.

Rosemary's hands tightly gripped the cup, oblivious of the heat it must be emanating. 'And how do you think their husbands react to that?' she asked tightly.

Brooke paused before answering, realising that Rosemary had at last decided to confide in someone. That it should be her Brooke was surprised to say the least, but maybe the other woman could talk to a stranger when she couldn't talk to a friend or her family. 'When a man and woman get married,' she replied slowly, taking care with her answer. 'They do exactly that, they marry *each other*.'

'But surely children are a natural progression from that?'

'Sometimes,' she nodded. 'But not always,' she added gently.

Rosemary gave a ragged sigh. 'Patrick wants children.'

It was a terse statement, and one that Brooke felt didn't require an answer, not yet.

'We went to an adoption society about a year ago,' Rosemary continued after a few minutes. 'Patrick wants a child so badly, and I thought I would be all right with a little baby——' she broke off, biting her bottom lip. 'Most couples want to adopt babies, it seems. There's a long waiting list. In fact, I'd almost begun to give up, when Patrick called me and told me they had a little girl for us to see.' She looked up with overbright eyes, tears hovering on the edge of her lashes. 'It was the afternoon I asked you to take care of Robert.'

Not a lover at all! 'I remember,' Brooke acknowledged quietly.

Rosemary swallowed hard. 'Patrick omitted to tell me the little girl was four years old! Oh, she was a pretty little thing,' she closed her eyes, the tears softly falling now, 'with black hair like mine, and lovely blue eyes. But she wasn't the baby I wanted, and I—I—I told the society I didn't think it would work out. Patrick asked them to let us think about it for a while, and I foolishly believed that would be the end of the matter. In the past,' her voice shook, 'I've always been able to talk Patrick round to my way of thinking. I thought an evening and night together in London and he would forget the whole thing. It didn't work out that way,' she choked. 'Patrick really liked the little girl, and he was adamant, either I give serious thought to adopting Sharon—that's her name—or our marriage was over.'

Brooke vividly remembered the other woman's brittle distress the evening she had arrived back from London so unexpectedly. And although she could sympathise with Patrick's wish for a child, she could also see that thrusting a child on Rosemary that she didn't want could be disastrous for everyone involved.

'I'm no good with young children,' Rosemary groaned her distress. 'I do try, but—You saw what I was like when Robert had mumps,' she sighed. 'I had no idea until I brought him here that he was even ill!'

'None of us realised, it wasn't just you. No woman

becomes a mother overnight,' Brooke soothed gently. 'It's something you grow into. What happened to Sharon's real parents?'

'They were killed in a car accident. You see, it wouldn't be like adopting a baby who knew no other parents; I just don't know if I could cope with the trauma Sharon's suffered,' Rosemary cried.

'Have you discussed all this with Patrick?' she frowned, sure that Patrick couldn't be this insensitive to his wife's confusion.

'Not really,' Rosemary sighed. 'He just seems to assume all women are born with maternal instincts, that all they need is a child to care for, any child,' she added bitterly.

'Then don't you think you should explain to him that he's wrong?'

Rosemary gave her a sharp look. 'Go up to London and see him, you mean?'

'Why not?'

She looked down at the cooling tea in the cup she still held. 'I'm not sure he wants to see me.'

'Isn't it worth finding out? Go and see him, Rosemary,' Brooke encouraged firmly. 'Don't let your marriage end because you're too proud to sit down and talk together.'

The other woman fell silent, obviously deep in thought, and Brooke moved tactfully to look out of the window to check on Robert. He was quite happily digging the bulbs out of the ground!

'I don't deserve to have you be nice to me,' Rosemary spoke suddenly, and Brooke turned back to look at her. 'I've been a bitch to you from the beginning.'

'You resented me,' she shrugged. 'You had a right to—I'm an interloper here.'

'Are you?'

Brooke raised cool brows questioningly. 'Of course.'

'I don't think so,' Rosemary shook her head. 'You've

made Rafe the happiest I've seen him since—for a very long time.'

Delicate colour entered her cheeks. 'I'm glad.'

Rosemary stood up. 'So am I. He loved Jacqui very much—You don't want to talk about his wife,' she dismissed tightly as Brooke paled. 'I do know that he cares more for you than I ever thought he would about a woman again.' She moved forward to hug Brooke. 'I thank you for that, and I thank you for helping me today. I'll go to London,' she straightened. 'It may not work out, but anything is better than being here without Patrick.'

'Yes,' Brooke answered abruptly, as she walked the other woman to the door, before going back into the cottage to sit down in the lounge.

Rosemary was the one, with her cruel barbs, who had convinced Jacqui that Rafe had never loved her. Now she claimed Rafe *had* loved his wife. Could Rafe have been telling her the truth last night when he claimed to have loved Jacqui very much?

And if he had been what could she do about it now? She was no longer Jacqui Charlwood, could never be her again, and she doubted Rafe would want her to be when he still believed she had had an affair with Greg Davieson. And although Rafe desired Brooke Adamson he certainly didn't love her!

CHAPTER NINE

'WHAT a little organiser you are,' Rafe drawled, turning from replacing the receiver on the telephone next to the bed. 'That was Rosemary,' he explained. 'She and Patrick have talked and it's been agreed with the adoption society that they have a trial period with Sharon.'

Brooke lay curled up against his side, both of them loath to get out of bed on this beautiful Saturday morning. It had been nice to wake beside him and know that he didn't have to dress and leave for work today, that they could be together all day if they wanted to. It was eleven o'clock already, and neither of them felt like making a move.

'I'm glad,' she murmured sleepily.

'Well, at least now I know what's going on,' he sighed as he put his arm about her shoulders. 'When Rosemary suddenly disappeared to London yesterday I wondered what had happened.' He grimaced ruefully. 'I should have known you'd had a hand in sorting it all out. You seem to be able to organise the whole family!'

'I can't organise you,' she taunted.

'Can't you?' he smiled down at her, an indulgent look in his eyes, a relaxed smile to his firm mouth.

Brooke still marvelled at this changed Rafe, knowing that even during the early days of their relationship four years ago that he hadn't been this relaxed with her, that in those days he had been reluctant to relax his guard in any way. But there were no pretences between them now, their physical relationship was perfect in every way.

She looked at him beneath lowered lashes. 'Can I?'

He moved convulsively towards her, shaking his head with a groan as he levered up and out of the bed. 'Remember we promised Robert we would take him out to lunch today.' He stood at the side of the bed, the expression of longing on his face telling her that lunch was the last thing on his mind at the moment.

Brooke gave him a mischievous smile, then slid out from beneath the sheets to face him, as naked as he. 'I've been looking forward to it.' She deliberately brushed her hip against him as she went to the bathroom.

'You little——!'

With a squeal of delight she ran into the bathroom and locked the door, hearing his muttered curses through the thickness of the wood. Rafe was fun like this, and she never wanted this closeness to stop, knowing that if the outside world ever intruded on them it surely would.

Robert was in his usually happy mood when he had the two of them together, and as always when they were together like this Brooke could imagine they were a real family. It was an exhilarating thought.

'Maybe we should get a slide and things put in over here for him,' Rafe drawled as Brooke rejoined him on the loungers in the garden later that afternoon, with Robert once again digging up her flowers. 'Or maybe we could bring the ones over from the house,' he turned to lace his fingers with hers, his thumb caressing the back of her hand. 'I have a feeling the two of us will be spending a lot of time over here in future. We may even move in—permanently.'

She swallowed hard, keeping her expression deliberately bland. 'Must I remind you that this is my cottage, Mr Charlwood?' she teased mockingly. 'You would have to be invited to stay before you moved in—permanently.'

The grey eyes were steady on hers. 'Well?'

She was the one to break the gaze, making a show

of watching Robert as he played. 'No permanence, no commitment, remember?' she said tightly.

'Brooke——'

'Let's not rush into something we could both regret.' She removed her hand from his, standing up to break the intimacy of the moment, knowing too well how badly she had been hurt by a seemingly permanent relationship between them once before. She would take what they had between them now, and would continue to live in this cottage when it was over.

Rafe's mouth firmed with displeasure at her evasion, but he didn't push the subject any further.

As he didn't during the next week, although their relationship continued to flourish. Rafe was a considerate and generous lover, often surprising her with small gifts she couldn't be insulted or take offence by, surprising her most of all when he insisted she be hostess at a small dinner party he was giving the following weekend.

She felt herself freeze as he made the suggestion, feeling mental and physical withdrawal as she recognised the names of the four married couples who were to be his guests. She had known them all as his friends when they lived together as man and wife. And his reason for introducing her to them as his hostess now completely baffled her.

'I'm proud of you,' he seemed to read her thoughts. 'I want to show you off to all my friends. Do you mind?'

What woman could genuinely mind such a compliment! But the thought of meeting those people at Rafe's side terrified the life out of her. She didn't want to become involved with the other aspects of his life; she liked the private world they had made for themselves at the cottage. Rafe still continued to spend every evening and night with her.

'You don't care for me enough to want people to know about us, is that it?' he rasped at her continued silence.

He was angry, but his anger no longer frightened her, and especially about something like this. He was hurt by her reluctance to be his hostess, and he showed that hurt by being angry. In her maturity she was slowly, belatedly, learning to know the man who had been her husband. He hid his real emotions behind a façade of arrogance and anger, but beneath the façade he was as vulnerable as the next man. And she had just injured his pride.

'Do you want me to wear anything in particular?'

Happiness flared in his eyes, making them look almost silver. 'Anything,' he said lightly. 'You look good in anything. Or nothing,' he added throatily, his eyes kindling with passion. 'I prefer you in nothing,' he groaned. 'I have fantasies about you all day long.'

'Poor Rafe!' she teased, leaning against his chest as they watched televison together.

'Lucky Rafe,' he corrected huskily. 'I get to put those fantasies into practice when we go to bed at night.'

'So *that's* where you get your ideas—Rafe!' she giggled as he turned to trap her beneath him on the sofa. 'Did you fantasise about this today?' she mocked.

'Every day.' His face was all hard planes in the light given off from the television, the rest of the room in darkness. 'I wish the hours away until I can get back to you.'

'Is this the same Rafe Charlwood of Charlwood Industries that all the newspapers claim is a workaholic?' She caressed the hardness of his jaw.

'Not any more.' His lips moved slowly over hers. 'I have a much better interest now, something—some*one* who absorbs me totally.'

'Me?'

'Can you doubt it?'

She couldn't doubt anything, not Rafe's growing love for her, or her own love for him, as he once again swept

her away on a tide of love so strong she forgot
everything but pleasing him in return.

The dinner party was going well; Brooke could see that,
could see it in the pride of Rafe's eyes every time he
looked at her. It was difficult for her not to flower
under the warmth of his attention, and yet still try to
remember the pain he had caused her in the past, to
keep their relationship in perspective. Especially as he
didn't leave her side all evening, making his claim on
her obvious to his guests, making her claim on him just
as obvious, not attempting to hide the pleasure he
found in just looking at her.

'It went well, didn't it?' he said softly as they sat
together once everyone had left, enjoying a quiet
brandy in the lounge.

She gave him a shy smile. 'Shouldn't I be the one
asking that?'

Rafe held her tightly to his side, his arm about her
shoulders. 'It wasn't a question, darling, it was a
statement. They all liked you very much.'

'Because I'm with you.'

'Because you're you,' he corrected firmly. 'You're
poised, confident, very warm and beautiful. How could
they help but like you?' he announced arrogantly.

She knew she had genuinely been accepted for herself
this evening, and unlike in the past she hadn't felt
threatened by Rafe's friends. Threatened? She brought
her thoughts up sharply. Is that really how she had felt
in the past, threatened? She knew it was, just as she
knew that tonight they had emerged from the privacy of
their relationship that she had feared so much and still
maintained their closeness. It had always been the
opposite in the past, Jacqui sensing that she was merely
tolerated because Rafe had been foolish enough to
marry her. In the light of the love he had confessed to
feel for his wife she wondered if she hadn't contributed

more to the breakdown of their marriage than she realised. She had always attributed the breakdown in communication between them to Rafe, had blamed all her past pain on him. To realise now that *her* youth, *her* uncertainty, *her* lack of confidence might have been part of the reason shocked her into silence. It had been so much easier when she could blame Rafe for everything!

'Brooke?' Rafe frowned his concern as she paled. 'Darling, what is it?'

She gave a bright smile that didn't reach her eyes. 'I think I'm just tired. It's been a long evening.' She put down her empty glass. 'I'd better go.'

He held her gaze with his. 'Stay.'

She shook her head stiffly. 'No!'

'Why not?' His frown returned.

She shrugged, standing up, her fingers laced together uncertainly. 'I just—I don't feel—comfortable being with you—here.'

'We can't hide for ever, Brooke.'

She raised startled eyes. 'What do you mean?'

He stood up in fluid movements, very dark and attractive in his black evening suit, a perfect foil for the lemon of her gown, her dark blonde hair secured loosely on top of her head, soft tendrils loose about her face and nape. 'Forget it for now,' his hand curled about her throat as he pulled her close to him, bending his head to gently possess her mouth with his. 'Let's go home,' he murmured huskily, a familiar fire burning in his eyes.

Home. Yes, the cottage was fast becoming that for them. A lot of Rafe's clothes were in the wardrobe beside her own, and most of his calls came there too now. And when the telephone rang early on Monday evening Brooke knew that it was probably for Rafe.

'Brooke?'

She instantly recognised Rosemary's voice, and from her light tone the other woman was very happy. 'How are you?' she returned warmly.

'Well. Very well,' Rosemary gave a light laugh. 'I don't think I'll ever make mother of the year, but I'm coping!'

Brooke mouthed the other woman's name to Rafe as he came through from the kitchen to check on the caller, having elected to cook their dinner tonight. She hadn't even realised he knew how to turn the cooker on, let alone cook with it! He gave a nod of acknowledgement before disappearing back into the kitchen.

'How are Patrick and Sharon?' asked Brooke.

'You don't know how good it sounds to hear their names grouped together like that,' Rosemary said huskily. 'It makes us almost seem like a proper family. I think we will be one day,' she added gravely. 'Sharon is still a little shy with us, but I think she'll come round in the end.'

'I'm glad.'

'So am I, glad I talked things out with you.' She gave a deep sigh. 'I've taken a good look at myself lately, and I haven't liked what I've found——'

'Rosemary——'

'No, let me finish, Brooke,' she said firmly. 'I may never have the courage to say this again. I'm not a very nice person, and when I—when I'm hurting myself I hit out at other people.'

'We all do that,' Brooke soothed the other woman.

'Yes,' Rosemary sighed. 'But sometimes I can be cruel, and—and not always truthful in my spite. I was like that with Jacqui.'

Brooke tensed, her hand tightly gripping the receiver. 'Oh?' she tried to sound casual, uninterested.

'When Rafe married her and brought her back to Charlwood I couldn't understand why he had married her—at first.' Rosemary gave another heavy sigh. 'It didn't take long for us all to realise how much in love with her he was. She was young, totally without guile—

and totally unaware of her power over Rafe. I wasn't kind to her at all, especially when she became pregnant.'

Brooke's tension had increased at this second insight into the events of four years ago from Rosemary. Why hadn't she realised at the time that Rosemary's bitchiness came from jealousy? Because she *had* been all the things Rosemary said she was, young, without guile, unaware of Rafe's deep love for her—she had also been stupid! She hadn't deserved Rafe's love then, had been too immature to understand it for what it was. And now it was too late, much too late.

'Brooke? Are you still there?' Rosemary's voice sharpened with concern. 'Have I upset you by talking about Rafe's wife?' she asked with regret.

'Yes,' Brooke answered truthfully.

'I'm sorry. I was only trying to explain—He cares for you very much, and I just wanted you to know the reason I was reacting to you as I did. It's nothing personal, I was just behaving jealously of someone else's happiness again.'

Brooke straightened, hardening herself to the fact that she had been more to blame for Rafe's cruelty in the past than he had, that she had destroyed his love for her by her lack of understanding about the way he felt. 'I think you may have misunderstood the situation between Rafe and myself,' she grated huskily. 'We're friends, but——' she broke off as a leanly tanned hand took the receiver from her, Rafe's expression hard as her lashes fluttered up nervously to look at him.

'Rosemary?' he rasped. 'Yes. Yes, I understand,' he glanced down at Brooke. 'Just leave well alone, hmm?' he added gently. 'Yes, I know.' He listened again as Rosemary talked. 'I'm sure she would like to. Robert can help her.' He rang off a few seconds later, looking down at Brooke wordlessly.

She couldn't meet that searching gaze, knowing he was angry about something.

Suddenly he came down on his haunches in front of her, grasping her hands painfully. 'We are friends, Brooke—I really hope that we're that,' he added fiercely. 'But we're lovers too. And that means that we're more than friends.'

She swallowed hard. 'Rosemary was talking about your wife, and——'

'Yes?' he prompted abruptly. 'Does it upset you to hear about Jacqui?'

'No.' She pushed past him to stand up. 'No, of course not. I just don't understand why everyone, you included, feels they have to keep explaining about your wife.' She was agitated by what she had just heard, becoming more and more convinced that Rafe *had* loved her. It was all such a mess, and if he should ever find out that she was Jacqui . . .! He would want to kill her for deceiving him. 'It's all in the past, isn't it,' she dismissed with a shrug.

Rafe's eyes were narrowed. 'As I remember it you held that past against me when we first met.'

She moistened her dry lips. 'I wasn't aware of all the facts then.'

'And are you now?'

She avoided his gaze. 'Not all of them, no.' But enough—oh yes, enough!

Rafe seemed to tense, his arms held stiffly at his sides. 'Would you like to be?' he asked softly.

Brooke turned away. 'No,' she bit out tautly. 'What did you tell Rosemary I would like to do, with Robert's help?' she changed the subject. 'It was me you were talking about, wasn't it?' she added lightly.

'Yes,' He thrust his hands into his pockets, dressed as casually as she in denims and a loose shirt. 'They're coming back to Charlwood at the weekend, and Rosemary wondered if you would supervise the decorating of the room next to theirs for Sharon. You could both drive up to London with me tomorrow and choose the wallpaper and things,' he encouraged.

It would be churlish to refuse, she knew that, as she nodded in agreement. But where was all this going to end?

'Doesn't it look nice?' Robert jumped up and down in his excitement.

The room they had prepared for Sharon did look nice, with Disney cartoon characters in the wallpaper, the cover on the quilt a lovely pale pink, as were the carpet and curtains, contrasting well with the snowy white nets and sheets. Rafe had bought several new toys for the arrival of his niece-to-be, and these had been put in the lovely toy box at the end of the bed.

Brooke and Robert were just giving the room a last-minute check as they waited for the arrival of Rosemary, Patrick and Sharon from London, mainly as a diversion for Robert; he was so excited about the prospect of a new cousin that he couldn't seem to stand still, had joined in with enthusiasm in the decorating of the room, often with disastrous results! His hair was an inch shorter on the top because paint had been cut from his hair on more than one occasion, several strips of wallpaper being ruined beyond redemption when he got to work on them with a pasting-brush, the actual paste itself being the one hazard Brooke had managed to keep him away from.

But the room had finally been completed yesterday, and the little boy's excitement was all for his new cousin now.

'I'm sure Sharon is going to love it.' Rafe had appeared in the open doorway without either of them being aware of it, very attractive in a fitted short-sleeved shirt of the very palest grey, and tailored trousers of charcoal grey. He walked over to put his arm about Brooke's shoulders. 'You've done a wonderful job,' he kissed her softly on the lips.

'Ugh!'

They both looked down at Robert in surprise, frowning at his grimace of distaste. 'What is it?' Rafe prompted his son.

'Do you like kissing and—and things?' he still grimaced.

Rafe was having difficulty holding back his smile of amusement. 'I'm afraid so,' he answered gravely.

Robert pulled a face. 'I think it's horrible! I won't ever let girls kiss me,' he announced indignantly.

Brooke could feel the vibration of Rafe's body as he tried to hold on to his laughter. 'Why don't you go downstairs and check that Cook has the lemonade ready for Sharon when she arrives?' she suggested.

'And me?' he asked hopefully.

'And you,' she nodded, smiling as he ran off down the stairs.

Rafe at last allowed his humour to show, laughing softly. 'Women will probably have to beat him off with a stick when he's older,' he mused, turning to mould Brooke against him, his hands linked loosely at the base of her spine.

'As they did you?' she teased, ecstatic that this wonderfully exciting and gentle man was her lover. It was becoming difficult to remember he had ever been cruel to her, ever denied her Robert, as he now shared their son with her completely.

'Maybe, when I was younger.' He sobered suddenly, his eyes a deep unfathomable grey. 'Actually, I'm glad you sent Robert downstairs, because there's something I wanted to talk to you about.'

Brooke instantly tensed. 'Yes?'

He drew in a steadying breath. 'Sharon is, by all accounts, a very sensitive little girl,' he began softly. 'She's been through a great deal already, and what she needs now is love and stability, on all levels.'

'Yes,' she nodded warily, not sure what he was leading up to.

'What I wanted to know was this,' Rafe voiced slowly. 'Shall I introduce you to her as my wife Jacqui, or would you rather I introduced you as my wife Brooke? Either name is fine as far as I'm concerned, but I think it would save confusion later if we were to decide——'

Brooke suddenly came out of the deep shock she had just received. 'You *know*?'

'Yes,' he spoke calmly. 'I know.'

CHAPTER TEN

SHE stared at his calm face in horror, trying to read from his expression; it remained enigmatic. 'You know,' she said again, nausea rising within her.

'Yes,' he nodded.

Brooke swallowed hard. 'H-How long? From the beginning?' Her eyes were wide, shocked.

'Not that long,' he answered gently. 'But for some time, yes.'

'God,' she choked. 'Oh God!' She turned on her heel with a wild cry of pain, fleeing the room, ignoring Rafe's call of her name as she ran down the stairs and out of the house. She stood outside for a moment not knowing where to go, galvanised into action as she sensed Rafe pursuing her, running to the only place she could go, the cottage. She knew Rafe was behind her now, she could almost feel his hot breath on her neck, and she groaned her relief as she reached the cottage and locked the door behind her, her eyes wide with terror as Rafe strode in through the front door.

'Brooke——'

She buried her face in her hands. 'What are you going to do to me?' she choked. 'I only wanted to be with Robert! I never wanted to hurt anyone. I only——'

'I know, I know,' Rafe soothed as he took her into his arms. 'I know all that you suffered to come back here.' His arms tightened convulsively about her, his breathing ragged against her cheek.

Brooke was crying too hard to take in anything he said, her worst fears realised. She was going to lose both Rafe and Robert for a second time! And this time,

176

no matter how much she had told herself she would accept it when her affair with Rafe ended, she didn't want to live, not even for Robert.

Rafe let her cry for several minutes, then he shook her gently. 'You'll make yourself ill,' he chided. 'Come on, Brooke, stop crying now.'

'I want to die!'

His fingers dug painfully into her arms. 'Don't talk like that,' his voice shook with emotion. 'Don't ever say anything like that again. I lost you once before, believed you were dead, I couldn't go on if it happened again!'

It took a long time for his impassioned words to penetrate her numbed brain, and even then she couldn't really believe she had heard them. Rafe wanted her out of his life—didn't he?

'If you can believe that,' he rasped, Brooke having spoken her thoughts aloud without realising it. 'After all that we've shared these past weeks, then I might as well be dead myself!' The last was spoken with desperation. 'Brooke, what we have, what we always had, is love. I love *you* more than life itself. And I've been hoping that you love me too,' the last was added uncertainly.

She couldn't answer him. 'What are you going to do with me?'

His arms slowly dropped away from her. 'Nothing,' he answered abruptly. 'What happens now is—is totally up to you.'

At last she looked at him, raising tear-wet lashes. Rafe looked haggard; there was a grey tinge to his face, his eyes were dark and haunted. 'What do you mean?' she asked nervously.

'I asked you a question a short time ago,' he reminded her softly, his gaze never leaving the pale beauty of her face. 'Which you haven't yet answered. Was it the decision about the names that you couldn't make, or whether or not you want to be my wife under any name?' the last came out harshly, his jaw rigid.

She swallowed hard. 'Why would you *want* me as your wife?'

'I just told you, I love you!' he rasped. 'Dear God, how I love you!' He rubbed his eyes as if they hurt him, his lashes as wet as hers now. 'When I began to want, to *need* Brooke Adamson as badly as I had once wanted Jacqui, I thought the nightmare was beginning all over again. I'd loved only once before in my life,' he continued gruffly as he knew he had her full attention. 'And it had been disastrous.'

'Jacqui?'

'You!' he corrected forcefully. 'I thought I was going out of my mind when you began to remind me of her— only your eyes and height seemed in the least similar. But the first time I kissed you, after Rosemary and Patrick's anniversary party, I knew I was falling in love again. And loving Jacqui, having her hate me, had almost destroyed me. I left you that night never intending to see you again. But I couldn't stay away from you for long. The night I returned to Charlwood and found you in the nursery after having spent the day with Robert it all looked so right to me, so natural.'

'I am his mother,' she reminded him bitterly.

'And you paid a harsh price to be with him,' Rafe said softly, the hand he had raised to touch her cheek falling abruptly away without making contact to be thrust into his pocket. 'I almost made love to you that night,' he continued flatly. 'And more and more you reminded me of Jacqui. I even called you by her name!'

'You told me that night that you'd hated your wife.'

A dark emotion flared in his eyes. 'Because she died and left me!'

Brooke shook her head. 'I'd left you long before that—I was pushed out. You wouldn't listen to me, let me explain about what you thought you'd seen with

Greg. You refused to talk to me, you took Robert away from me,' she reminded him bitterly. 'Those aren't the actions of a man who loves but of a man who hates. I knew I was a disappointment to you once I became your wife, that I was young and silly, and had no idea how your wife should behave. I rebelled at the mould you pushed me into. But you could have helped me overcome all that if you'd once shown me you loved me——'

'*Shown* you?' he gasped disbelievingly. 'That was the one thing I did do, even though I might not have said the words. I slept, dreamed, *lived* my love for you. You were never out of my thoughts, I always wanted you in my arms, making love with me. But you began to withdraw from me, grew dissatisfied with our life together, longed for the excitement of the life you'd lived in London before we met——'

'That isn't true,' she snapped, beyond caring, knowing that all the pain and bitterness of the past had to come out now. 'Once we moved to Charlwood you suddenly stopped being Rafe and became the head of the Charlwood household. I became another Charlwood possession, to be taken out and displayed every so often and forgotten about in between those times.'

'That's a lie,' Rafe rasped. 'I never wanted anyone else to even look at you. I resented those occasions when we had to be with other people, I thought a child would bind you to me for ever. But when he was born I resented even his claim on your time, I wanted you all to myself.'

Her eyes narrowed at his obvious sincerity. 'You treated me like a possession, not a wife. You never once told me you loved me.'

'It was obvious to everyone——'

'Not me!'

Rafe drew in a ragged breath. 'I loved you so much it made me weak. I thought——'

'I would take advantage of that weakness,' she realised dully.

'Yes!' he was breathing harshly. 'Yes,' he repeated more calmly.

Her mouth twisted. 'You loved me so much you didn't even go to America to identify my body!'

Rafe shuddered with reaction. 'I couldn't,' he said shakily. 'I couldn't bear the thought of seeing you all broken and torn, so still, no life left in your beautiful blue eyes. Just the thought of it gave me nightmares. I had to drink myself into oblivion for months afterwards just to block my imaginings from my mind.'

'I wouldn't have been in America at all if you hadn't thrown me out of your life, taken Robert away from me!'

'I was wrong to do that, but once it had started I couldn't seem to stop it. You seemed to be having an affair with Greg Davieson, and just the thought of that——'

'I visited the girls in Sensuous Romance, not him!'

'I couldn't accept that, I thought that every man who saw you had to want you as much as I did. And with your unhappiness with me I thought you just might want them too.'

'I've had only one lover in my life, Rafe,' she told him coldly. 'Then and now.'

He gave a ragged sigh. 'I was jealous——'

'You could have talked to me! How could I hope to explain myself when you wouldn't even *talk* to me?'

His hands shook as he ran them through the thickness of his hair. 'Even then I couldn't tell you how much I loved you. I thought you would beg me through the lawyers to come back,' he revealed huskily. 'If only to be with Robert.'

'*That's* why you refused access to him?' she gasped.

Rafe nodded abruptly. 'I believed our son would bring you back to me even though you no longer loved me. Instead you went to America—and as I thought, died there.' There was still pain in his eyes as he recalled the deep shock he had received when he had been told of her death. 'I loved you—but at that moment I hated you too. You'd gone from me for ever, and all I had left was a vacuum, long empty years without you. I wanted no other woman after that, I barely noticed their existence, until Brooke Adamson began to visit Jocelyn.' He looked at her with shadowed eyes. 'For the first time in three years I began to feel interest in a woman again, to look forward to the occasional glimpses I would have of you with my aunt.'

'You always gave the impression you never noticed me,' Brooke said dully, suddenly feeling weak and sitting down abruptly.

'I didn't *want* to notice you,' he revealed raggedly. 'It seemed like a betrayal of what I felt for Jacqui. But my desire for you became so strong, so forceful that I knew I had to do something about it. I convinced myself that it would only be a physical thing, that my emotions would never become involved again.'

'You propositioned me.'

'And you promptly turned me down,' he recalled dryly. 'Went on to tell me I was vicious and cruel to have denied my wife her son,' he added deeply. 'I *was* vicious and cruel, but it was one of those mistakes I'd told you I made in my marriage that were difficult to undo. I had loved you, but you seemed bored with both the marriage and me, I thought the only way to keep you was through Robert. Instead you chose to fight me publicly for him——'

'When I should have begged to come back,' she finished raggedly. 'You'd never given any indication that you wanted me back—under any conditions. I thought you'd only married me in the first place to provide you with your son.'

'Rosemary,' he sighed.

Her eyes widened. 'You know—what she said to me that day when I left the house?'

He nodded. 'When you were supposedly killed her conscience got the better of her, and she confessed that she'd been responsible for your going to the studio as you did.'

Brooke shook her head. 'I don't think that's strictly true,' she denied quietly. 'If I'd been more sure of you, of our marriage, I wouldn't have been affected by anything she told me.'

Rafe drew in a ragged breath. 'Probably not. I don't think Jocelyn was ever sure of my feelings for you either. She was furious with me for treating you the way I did, and refused to come to the house for months afterwards. That's probably the reason she never knew of the way I had to drink myself into a drunken stupor just to get myself through the nights without you.'

'You began drinking *then*?'

'Without you I had nothing. And it was too late to get you back; you couldn't stand me as your husband even for Robert's sake,' he recalled bitterly. 'I doubt you had much trouble persuading Jocelyn to help you after your accident; she always believed in your innocence, always disapproved of the way I'd treated you. She never forgave me for that.'

'But she loved you,' Brooke told him gently. 'She only agreed to help me after the doctor told her I was on the edge of a complete nervous breakdown, that I could even die.'

'Because of what I'd done to you?'

'Yes.'

'God!' he groaned his despair.

'Rafe, when did you know Brooke Adamson was Jacqui?' She looked at him anxiously.

A smile softened his lips. 'I'd been aware of— something about you for some time, but I was certain that night I got back from Australia and we made love.

I could never ever mistake your lovemaking for anyone else's,' he admitted huskily. 'I began to hope that night too, knew that if you *were* Jacqui that you couldn't hate me and still make love with me like that. I sent Patrick to America to find out the truth——'

'That's where he went?' she gasped—then another thought suddenly occurred to her. 'It was he who telephoned the cottage that night!'

'Yes,' he nodded. 'That was when I truly began to believe in miracles. It seemed I'd been given a second chance with you, one I *had* to take. I knew your reason for being here had to be because of Robert; your interest in his welfare was enough to convince me of that. And with that knowledge, the sacrifice you'd made of your beautiful face, the way you'd told me you loved your husband more than life itself, came the final conviction that Greg Davieson had never meant anything to you. The woman—child, I had thought you to be would never have gone through what you have to be with her son.'

'You—you don't like the new me?' She put up a hand self-consciously to her face.

'I *love* every part of you, the old you and the new one. You were beautiful then and you are now. But it wouldn't matter to me what you look like, I love *you*, the inside you. Doesn't the fact that I recognised your soul, despite your changed appearance, tell you that?' he groaned.

'I thought it was my body you recognised?' She attempted to lighten the mood, at last beginning to believe in a love she had doubted for so long, the love that had driven him to cruelty, to himself as much as to her.

Rafe smiled stiffly. 'That too,' he admitted ruefully. 'These last few weeks we've been together have been heaven to me, and I know you couldn't have responded so openly to me if you hated me completely. I've tried to be more open with you this time, to show you how I feel. Last time I was so full of cynicism and reserve that when I fell in love and married you I wasn't sure how to cope with it. I know, I know,' he sighed at her disbelieving expression. 'I always gave the impression of being self-sufficient. I was until I met you. And then I was so much in love I didn't know what to do about it. I was so busy trying to hide from you how deeply I felt about you that I didn't realise you needed my support, to be shown that love. I hope the last few weeks have, in part, helped to ease some of the pain I've caused you. If they haven't I don't know what I'll do—I can't bear it if you leave me again!' The last came out as a desperate plea.

'So Patrick knows the truth about me,' she said thoughtfully. 'Was he shocked?'

'Stunned, as I was,' Rafe corrected softly. 'And proud too, when he realised how brave you've been the last three years. As I am.'

'Then Rosemary knows too?'

'Yes,' he frowned at these questions. 'Patrick told her when she joined him in London.'

'Which is why she tried to talk to me about the past last weekend.'

'Yes.'

'Then I think Brooke, don't you?' she said casually.

'Brooke what?' Rafe frowned his puzzlement.

'Brooke your wife,' she looked at him with all the love she had inside her, a love that had never quite been able to die. 'In a way Jacqui did die, and I think she should stay that way. I'm a different person now, but I'd like to be your wife again. Oh, Rafe, I love you,' she went gratefully into his arms. 'I love you so much! I didn't know what was going to happen,' she held on to him tightly. 'I hated you for such a long time, and then I suddenly realised that beneath the hate I loved you too. I was so mixed up for a time that I didn't know what I was doing, all I knew was that I loved you.'

'Darling!' He rained fevered kisses over her throat and face. 'Darling . . .!' His mouth claimed hers in a kiss that drew the very soul from her body, but gave his in return.

'I hate to interrupt . . .?'

They both turned to look at Patrick as he stood in the open doorway, the ecstatic expression on their faces telling a story of their own.

'Jacqui . . .?' he prompted softly.

She ran to him with a happy laugh, hugging him briefly. 'I prefer Brooke now, but I'll forgive you for the lapse this time. Are Rosemary and Sharon at the house?'

'Yes. Robert seemed to think you might be over here,' he grinned, looking more relaxed and happy than Brooke could ever remember him being before. 'Kissing and things, I think was the way he described it,' he added tongue in cheek.

'Little devil!' Rafe joined them, his arm going about Brooke's shoulders as she leant back against him, a look of total love and possession in his face.

'He was right, though, wasn't he,' Patrick mocked. 'Welcome back, Brooke,' he spoke to her gently. 'I'll expect you over at the house in a moment; I'd like you both to meet my daughter.'

'We'll be there in a few minutes.' Rafe squeezed his shoulder gratefully, and the door closed softly behind Patrick seconds later. 'I'll make everything right for us, Brooke.' He turned her into his arms. 'I promise you I won't let anything ever part us again.'

'Will we move back into Charlwood?' she asked.

His eyes softened understandingly. 'Not if you don't want to. We can stay here. In fact, I quite like the life we have together here.'

'So do I,' she touched his face lovingly. 'And it will be nice to come here and spend a few days together when we feel like being alone. But I think our place is in the main house. I've changed, Rafe, I've grown up. I'm no longer afraid of who or what you are. And I'll never allow what happened to us before to happen again.'

'My tigress!' he said half teasingly, half admiringly.

'Your wife, Rafe Charlwood!' she smiled up at him. 'And don't you ever forget it.'

'You think I would ever want to?' he groaned.

She knew he wouldn't, knew of his deep love for her and valued it above everything else. 'I'll always love you, Rafe,' she promised him.

'As I will always love you.'

As they walked back to the house together hand in hand Brooke knew that the man at her side would always be exactly that in future, by her side.

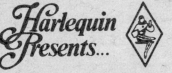

4 FREE
Harlequin Romances

Harlequin Photo Calendar

Turn Your Favorite Photo into a Calendar.

Uniquely yours, this 10 x 17½" calendar features your favorite photograph, with any name you wish in attractive lettering at the bottom. A delightfully personal and practical idea!

Send us your favorite color print, black-and-white print, negative, or slide, any size (we'll return it), along with **3** proofs of purchase (coupon below) from a June or July release of Harlequin Romance, Harlequin Presents, Harlequin Superromance, Harlequin American Romance or Harlequin Temptation, plus $5.75 (includes shipping and handling).